I0552259

Old Family Mansion

Haunted Quest, Volume 1

Jenni Leigh

Published by Prudence MacLeod, 2024.

Old Family Mansion
by Jenni Leigh
Copyright, March 01/2014
(second edition)
(previously published under the Prudence MacLeod name)

OLD FAMILY MANSION

First edition. January 23, 2024.

Copyright © 2024 Jenni Leigh.

ISBN: 978-1927478578

Written by Jenni Leigh.

Last Will and Testament of a Right Bastard

The five young men sat uneasily in the waiting room of the law offices. They were strangers but bore an odd resemblance to each other. They made uneasy conversation until the secretary came to usher them into the opulent private office. Behind the desk sat a tall balding man in his sixties. His smile of greeting was reminiscent of the grim reaper.

"Be seated gentlemen," he said, a hint of glee in his voice. "I've arranged to have you all meet here for the first time to receive your inheritance. I must tell you; I have never encountered anything like this in all my years of practicing law. Please bear with me. I will first show you a video recording of a man's will. He will explain everything to you in the recording. Afterwards we will take care of the official paperwork."

He finished the speech and turned away from the men to picked up a remote control. A piece of the wall slid away, and a large screen TV was revealed. "This was recorded three weeks before the old gentleman's death due to heart failure."

The camera moved in until the old man's face filled the screen. He coughed slightly and began to speak. "Greeting gentlemen, my name is Malcom Miller. I'm your grandfather, and this is my story.

"I was born to wealth and power, an only child. I grew up to be a monster, a right bastard so I've been called many times. I've ruined

1

many a man in my quest for wealth, and I did it to watch them fall. Yes, I know I'm bound for hell. I'm actually looking forward to the challenge." He chuckled but his laugh turned into a rough, hacking cough.

At length, he recovered his breath and continued. "Forgive me. Let me continue. I will now explain how you all came to be related, and why you're all here. In my thirties, I became upset and devised the most diabolical plan. I'd find a way to torture the next generation of men in the family, to make them earn their inheritance, so this is what I did.

"You see, in an attempt to guarantee a male heir, I went to five different small towns outside the city and impregnated a woman in each place, a surrogate mother of sorts. I made certain they were comfortable in life because it was their children I wanted, not them. Sadly, I didn't get my male heir, all I got was daughters.

So here you are, each the only grandson of one liaison. Now is when we get to the fun part. I've taken certain steps over the years to make sure you don't meet until this day. This is where I bust your balls for having the wrong mothers, or you beat me at my own game proving yourselves worthy of the bloodline.

"Why? Because I'm a bastard, as I said." He cackled again, and again it turned to a lung dredging cough. Eventually he was able to go on.

"So, it comes to this. Each woman lived in a certain area. In each of these areas I bought an old property. I've left one property to each of you. I did live a few months in each of the properties, but each has been abandoned for many years. Eventually I let the taxes lax, so time is running out. All this is deliberate to make your lives much harder.

"In each of these properties I've left a riddle and a piece of a map. Complete the map, figure out the clues, gentlemen, and you will be wealthy beyond your wildest dreams. Fail and it all rots forever in the bank vaults.

"I know each and every one of you. I've kept tabs on you all your lives. So now it comes down to you against me. Can you unravel the twisted trail I've left for you, or will you number among the hundreds I've left begging on the streets?" He dissolved into another laughing/coughing fit.

The old man regained his breath and faced the camera again. "Be it known that this is the last will and testament of myself, Malcom Alvin Miller, being of sound mind and failing body. I do hereby leave my entire fortune to my five grandsons provided they can unravel the puzzle I have set for them. Good luck, gentlemen; you're going to need it." He cackled and coughed again as the camera faded to black.

"Rotten son of a bitch," said one young man. "So that's why Gran would never speak of Grandpa."

"Yes, he was," agreed another, "and he was damned proud of it."

"So what's it going to be, guys?" asked a deep voice. The speaker was the smallest of them at barely five foot ten, but he was hard muscled and lean. He looked like he could be dangerous. "This looks like an all or nothing deal. Do we go for it, or do we go home?"

"I say we do it, spoil the old bastard's fun," said another.

"I say we need more information," said another. Jace Harper was the eldest and most sober looking of them all. "If I read this right, there's a lot more going on here. For example, he said he'd let the taxes go. I'll bet it'll take every cent we've got to bail out these properties."

"Yeah, and maybe the old bugger died broke anyway," said another.

"Gentlemen," interrupted the lawyer, "I can assure you there is a prize available, as I am the executor of this will. There is a sum, after all appropriate taxes and fees, of approximately two hundred and seven million dollars. Liquidate all hard assets and you can easily double that. However, you must all work together, trust each other, and all arrive here together with the solution to claim the prize."

"All right," said deep voice, "I say we do this. Any objectors?"

"I'm in," came several replies, all except one. They all turned to look at the silent one, Jace Harper.

"Well? Are you in or not?" asked Deep Voice.

Slowly the silent one rose to his feet and made eye contact with each of the others. "All right, think about this for a minute. This can't be done half-assed. That old man had a seriously twisted mind. We're not going to walk into an old building and find a note pinned under the kitchen drawer. This won't be easy, and it could take years if it can be done at all.

"We have to trust each other completely, be worthy of that trust, and work together, help each other if we can. Are you all willing to do that? Will you still be so enthusiastic two years of frustration from now? Think for a minute before you jump into this madness.

"Do you actually believe everything the old bugger said? I don't. I think he's already thrown a few red herrings into the mix. To do this we have to put our heads together and often. It'll take the lot of us to figure this out, if we ever can."

"So I repeat the question," grinned Deep Voice. "Are you in or not?"

"I guess we're related after all," Jace sighed in response. "You're all as crazy as I am. I'm in."

There was a round of laughter at that. "All right, we're ready," said Jace, as he turned to face the lawyer, "give us the bad news."

"Actually, I have both bad news and good. Your benefactor didn't want the need to earn a living interfere with the quest, so he has provided $250,000 each. However, you must sign a binding agreement that you will not take a paying job or contract ever again in this lifetime.

"Jace Harper, sign here, and here please." Jace turned back and looked at the others once again. They all nodded their agreement. He leaned on the expansive desk and signed. "Thank you, and here is the deed to your new property. Good hunting."

The lawyer witnessed the signature then reached for another folder. "Mr. Ira Dunbar please. The young mountain of muscle ran his fingers through his golden hair then stood and signed the papers. They all followed in turn.

As they left the law office each man held an envelope containing copies of the agreement, a printout of the text of the will, a check for a quarter million dollars, and the deed to a property he'd never seen. Each also had only a week to quit his job.

"There's a coffee shop just down the street," said Ira, as they entered the elevator. "Let's go put our heads together."

"I'd rather go for a beer," rumbled Deep Voice.

"I wouldn't," said Jace. "Think about it, cousin."

"I am. I'm thinking I have fifty bucks in my pocket and a check for a quarter mil in my hand."

"Yeah, and you just signed a deal to never take a job again, ever," replied Ira.

"How long do you think that quarter mil will last if you go on a bender?" asked Jace.

"Probably about two weeks," chuckled Deep Voice. "All right, looks like I'm on the wagon. Once we solve this damn thing I fully intend to celebrate."

"I'll help you," chuckled another. "I'm Logan Kerry."

"Morgan Ross," replied Deep Voice, as he offered his hand.

"Aiden Reilly," added the tallest, as he too, offered his hand.

The introductions were finished as they reached the ground floor and filed out to the street. There was a bank across from the law office and they all entered, opened accounts, and deposited the checks. From there they retired to the coffee shop to make plans.

As they entered, Jace bought five maps and brought them to the table. "Okay guys, I'm thinking we should move into these properties, as we'll need to protect them, search for clues and, well, we aren't exactly going to have money coming in for rent. So, everybody mark his new town, address, and cell number on all the maps, then we'll all know where everybody is."

"Good thinking," said Morgan as he carefully followed the directions. "You've been thinking ever since we walked into that lawyer's office; I could hear the wheels turning. I say we make you the official coordinator for this operation."

"That makes sense," agreed Ira. "Jace seems to be the sharpest tool in our collective shed. I vote yes." The others agreed.

"All right, guys, I'll do my best here," said Jace. "However, there's not a lot any of us can do at first. First we have to find the pieces of the map and we're all on our own with that. Once somebody finds his piece he puts it in a safe deposit box then goes to help one of the others. As soon as we have all the pieces we get together and work as a team from there."

"Good thinking," said Logan. "How about we get together about once a month for a progress report." It was agreed. They finished their coffee, wished each other luck, and then set out on each individual treasure hunt.

One week later, in a small town outside the city...

Mara O'Grady rose early and pulled on her jeans. She washed up, then combed out her nut brown hair and tied it back in a ponytail. Today was the day. She'd promised herself that she would become less fearful and more adventurous after she turned thirty. Her birthday was two months past.

She pulled on a plaid shirt then checked herself in the full length mirror by the bedroom door. "What the hell are you doing?" she muttered at her reflection. "A push-up bra? Are you trying to be sexy? Sexy is for girls five foot ten and a hundred pounds, not women over thirty, five foot five and a hundred and forty." She sighed and let her shoulders droop.

"Oh to hell with that," she hissed fiercely at the doomsayer of a reflection. She straightened her back and thrust out her chest. Hand on hip, she gave a little wiggle. "This girl's got curves and they look fine." With a regal toss of her head, she stepped into her boots and laced them snug.

Stopping at the mirror by the door, Mara gazed wistfully at her reflection for a moment. It was to be a day of doom, destiny, and bright new beginnings, a day of misadventures. She shook off the moment and stepped through the door to face whatever might come.

A few moments and a brisk walk in the morning sun later she was having breakfast with her friends at the café.

A New World

"**M**ara O'Grady," laughed the tiny waitress, as she hurried over to the foursome of women who were her best customers and her closest friends, "aren't you working today?"

"Of course I'm working today, Arlene." smiled the woman in the horn rimmed glasses, as she adjusted them on her nose. "Why would you ask a thing like that?"

"Oh, I don't know," grinned Arlene, as she poured the coffee then slid into the booth with them. "Maybe it's the plaid shirt and jeans instead of the hair in a bun and the black dress you always wear to work."

"And look, she's wearing a ponytail too," said Meghan O'Grady, Mara's sister.

"Oh stop, all of you," she smiled. "If you must know, today is the day I begin my new career."

"What?" exclaimed the girl with the multicolored hair. "You're leaving the library?"

"I most certainly am not leaving the library," replied Mara. "I plan to expand it."

"You really are going to try to get a museum started attached to the library?" asked her sister.

"I already have the go ahead from the town, and the library has plenty of space in the basement to get it started."

"So, what sorts of things are you going to put in there, Mara?" asked Arlene.

"I want each piece to have a bit of the town's history attached to it. Today I'm going to have a look at the old Miller mansion on the hill."

"You're not," exclaimed Meghan. "Mara, that old place is a death trap. Besides, it's haunted."

"Be that as it may, that's this morning's agenda."

"My sister, the tomb raider," sighed Meghan. "Happy hunting. If you're not back by dark I'll send out the search party."

Mara endured their gentle teasing with grace and a smile then headed for the library.

As she walked in, her volunteer assistant, her Aunt Louise, looked her over and raised an eyebrow. "We have new uniforms now?" she asked, absently brushing a lock of her long silvery hair back from her face. "I'm sorry, Mara. I didn't get the memo."

"Very funny, Aunt Louise," replied Mara, trying not to laugh as she headed for her desk. "Just for that I'm leaving you on your own this morning."

"I'll try to keep the hordes at bay. Mara O'Grady, what are you up to?"

"I'm going exploring up at the old Miller place this morning."

"Whatever for?"

"We want to get a museum started," replied Mara, "and I want to write the history of Higgston. That place has been empty for as long as I can remember. It has to be full of history relating to this town."

"That's private property, Mara. You could get in trouble, not to mention breaking your neck falling through a rotten floor."

"Aunt Louise, there hasn't been a caretaker in that cottage for years. The place is abandoned; nobody will ever know I was there."

Louise turned back to her task of replacing books on the proper shelves. "What possessed you to attempt this madness anyway?" She asked as she worked.

"It was an article in one of the old newspapers we keep in the archives. I was researching the history when I found the reference. Apparently, the Millers maintained an extensive library. I'd like to get a look at it," smiled Mara, as she closed the drawer of her desk. She'd found the flashlight she'd been looking for, as well as a large notepad and a pen. Mara fully intended to make notes, lots of them. "Hold down the fort," she called, as she headed for the door."

"You be careful, Mara," called Louise, but Mara was already gone.

Trespasser

M ara loved to hike in the warm sun, and this was a perfect day for it. She marched past her car and headed for the old mansion on the hill overlooking Higgston. She was sweating lightly and breathing deeply, both with the exertion as well as the excitement.

As she neared her target she began to lose some of her bravado. The old driveway was cracked and heaved up by too many winters. The grass had reclaimed much of it. The once vast perfectly groomed lawns were long since overgrown and returned to wild fields, scattered with small trees.

The once well-tended bushes that hugged the house had gone wild. The roses had claimed a large area just at the main door of the house making it somewhat impossible to approach. Mara skirted the now wild roses and searched for a back entrance. She noticed the peeling paint but was heartened by the fact the windows seemed to be intact. If the roof had held then there should be minimal damage inside.

Mara found the path to the back door still clearly visible. The old caretaker had been unable to do much maintenance is his last few years, but had obviously still tried to keep the place up. This must have been how he accessed the house. She looked over her shoulder and saw the caretaker's cottage at the bottom of the property on the side street. The path was unused recently, but still clearly visible leading down to the cottage.

As Mara climbed the steps, there came a strong impression of danger and she shivered. Something clearly didn't want her to enter. However, there seemed to be another spirit behind the first one, begging her to bring life back inside the old house. She took another step and the sense of foreboding grew stronger.

"So," she breathed softly, "there is something inside worth guarding after all. Well you can give me the creeps all you want; I'm still going in." She tried the door and found it unlocked. Closer inspection showed where it had been pried open. "I guess I'm not the first to explore the old place."

The door opened to a large room that had obviously been a back porch and a servant's entrance. She passed through into a large kitchen from another era. It was interesting and exciting, but not what she was after. Mara continued on. She passed through the kitchen and into the once formal dining groom. The sunlight through the dirty windows showed the layers of dust that lay on the sheets that covered everything. She moved on through the dining room and into a wide hallway. The large sliding doors across the hall revealed the living room so she closed them again. Perhaps the library would be on the second floor.

The main foyer was large with a curved staircase leading to the second floor. She went up, but found only four bedrooms, each with private bath. All had been untouched for ages. Mara went back to the first floor where she found two more rooms leading off the main living room. One was a large private study with a fireplace, mahogany desk, several leather chairs and loaded bookcases.

Another door led from the study and she opened that to find her prize; a two story library much bigger than the one in town where she worked. This was what she had dreamed of. Covering her face with her scarf, Mara took up the old feather duster from the large center table and set to work, starting on the second floor. The day was well on, and it was near dusk when, tired and famished, Mara descended to the first floor.

As her foot touched the floor, she heard the engine and saw the car parking at the gate. She watched through the window as a tall man climbed out, took a look at the house, then pulled a machete from the back seat, and headed up the lane out of sight.

Frozen it terror, Mara didn't move for several moments, and then it was too late. The man was in the house. Maybe if she was really quiet he wouldn't find her. Wrong. She could hear him moving about the ground floor, but he didn't go upstairs to give her a chance to make an escape. No, slowly but surely his footsteps grew closer until she knew she was trapped. Suddenly he stepped through a door she hadn't seen before. He was still holding the machete.

Her father had often said that the best defense was an all-out full frontal attack. Mara gave it a try.

"Who are you? What are you doing here?" she demanded, as he spotted her at the foot of the stairs.

He was tall with sandy brown hair and a three day scruff of beard. He was also dressed in clothes that suggested he had just bought them. This man looked as though he'd be more comfortable in a suit and tie. His eyes had gone hard as flint at sight of her, but they softened and a small grin began to play at the corners of his mouth. "I'm Jace Harper," he said, as he let his eyes roam over her figure appreciatively. "I own the place. Who are you? What are you doing here?"

"My name is Mara O'Grady," she replied, as a blush touched her cheeks and her glasses slid down her nose. She pushed them back into place. "I suppose you could say I'm trespassing."

Moving On

Since the distances weren't all that great, the five cousins decided to meet in Jace's new town once each month. They went their separate ways and Jace was lost in thought as he drove the highway home. It was dark when he arrived back at his apartment. He pulled a plate of cold meat and warmed it in the microwave.

"All right, Jace my boy," he mused as he sat to his meager meal, "just what the hell have you gotten yourself into this time?"

"Well, let's see; I have to quit my job, kiss a promising career goodbye, go live in an old abandoned house in a strange town, and worst of all I have to find a clue and a map in that place before I even consider selling it. Oh yeah, let's not forget all the back taxes the old bastard let go. Damn his evil eyes.

"All right, Jace, stop whining and start working. It's time to make a to-do list." With his usual practical work ethic, Jace began a list of things to do to close out his affairs. He finished his list and began packing. Eventually he had to stop and try to sleep, but sleep was elusive. His mind continued to race over what had happened and what he was facing.

Jace gave up and rose early to continue packing. At nine he stopped off at a thrift store and donated all his suits, except for the navy. That would do for weddings and funerals. He arrived at the office dressed in jeans and a T-shirt. He smiled at the stares he was getting. At least there would be one moment of fun in all this madness.

"Mr. Harper, what do you think you're doing?" puffed a balding man, as he marched from the inner office bearing down on Jace.

"Cleaning out my desk," came the reply. "Here, this is for you, Mr. Efford." Jace placed an envelope addressed to him in his hands.

"What is this?"

"My resignation, effective yesterday."

"You have to give notice; you can't just leave like this."

"Watch me," replied Jace, as he hit the delete button to clear off the computer he used. He picked up the small box of belongings and headed for the door.

"You hit the lottery, Jace?" asked one woman.

"Nope, just cracked under the stress," he chuckled in reply, as he exited the building.

Once outside he tossed the box into the back seat of his car and got in. "All right, smart ass," he muttered, "you've had your fun, now get busy before you totally freak out and self-destruct."

Keeping busy was an easy way to keep his mind off what he'd just done. Jace had set out to be a *somebody* even before he left high school. He kept his nose to the grindstone all through university and had worked for the same company ever since. At thirty-two, Jace was still living like a hermit, but he'd managed to pay off all his student debts as well as the debts his father had left behind.

To his practical mind, what he'd just done was akin to suicide. By the end of the day he had put all his belongings in storage, traded his car for an older model, then set out for Higgston and his date with destiny. He stopped at a motel that night, and after a meal at the café he returned to his room and opened a bottle of whiskey.

By one a.m. he'd managed to empty the bottle, his stomach contents, and quieted his mind. His last thought before falling asleep was, *"I'd better not let Morgan find out about this."*

Jace spent the next day in the motel, sulking and nursing the worst hangover of his life. The following morning he set out once again. He stopped first to eat, then to buy a few basic tools from a hardware store. He also bought a machete. An old abandoned place was bound to be overgrown.

He arrived in town mid-afternoon and stopped in at the café for a meal and directions. The tiny waitress with the bright smile gave him a strange look as she directed him to the old run down mansion on the hill overlooking the town.

As Jace pulled up and parked the car he thought he saw someone at the window. "Great," he muttered, climbing out of the old car, "right off the bat I've got burglars or ghosts." Catching sight of the rose bushes blocking the door he pulled out the machete.

Picturing himself as a knight using a sword to slash through the thorns surrounding a castle, he waded into the rosebushes. "All right now," he breathed as he inserted the key in the lock and wrestled the front door open. A feeling of great foreboding came over him, but he shook it off. "Too late for that crap now. Let's go see who's in here, damsel or dragon."

Jace easily spotted the tracks in the dust. "Small boots, that bodes well for a damsel," he grinned to himself. "Okay, she went up, but came back down. Now where did she go? Living room, yeah and there are her tracks leading to the study and the library. She hasn't come back out yet. It must have been her I saw at the window. Now, if I remember the floor plan right, there should be another door to the library. Maybe I can sneak up on her. Too bad she's got a guy with her though."

It took him only a few moments to find the second door and push his way through. What he saw as he entered took his breath away for a moment. She was standing at the base of the stairs, a feather duster in her hand and the fading rays of sunlight dancing on her hair like a halo. The girl was all delicious curves and had large liquid brown eyes with the longest lashes he had ever seen. Jace took a moment to appreciate the vision before him. And then she spoke in a demanding voice.

"Who are you? What are you doing here?"

"I'm Jace Harper and I own the place," he replied, with a grin. "Who are you and what are you doing here?"

"I'm Mara O'Grady," she replied, blushing softly. "I guess I'm trespassing."

Trespassers

"Yes, Ma'am, you certainly are," replied Jace.

"Please don't call the police," she begged. "I didn't take anything."

"I believe you, Mara, is it? I believe you, Mara, but what about your boyfriend?"

"Boyfriend? I don't have a boyfriend. What are you talking about?"

"Look at the floor, girl. There's the proof of the lie. Those small footprints in the dust are yours, but just who made the big tracks beside them?"

"You did."

"Nope. I came through this door back here, there are my tracks. No my dear, there were two of you."

"No, I came alone," she replied, her eyes pleading with him to believe. Gazing into those eyes, Jace was ready to believe anything she wanted to tell him.

With Jace momentarily entranced, the man hiding behind a bookcase made his break. He blasted from behind the case, shoulder blocked Jace into the wall, and fled. Jace gave chase, but the man was well ahead of him. He could only watch helplessly from the back door as the man raced down the hill, past the cottage, and leaped into a car.

"Son of a bitch," swore Jace, as he hurled the machete after the fleeing bandit.

"He got away, huh?"

Jace bit back his first response. "Yeah, he did," he sighed. "On the bright side he didn't look to be carrying anything."

"I wonder why he ran away?"

"Maybe he didn't want to be arrested for trespassing."

"Oh, that," she said, not making eye contact. "Maybe he's just another treasure hunter."

"Like you?"

"I doubt that," Mara replied rather tartly.

"Well, if you're not a treasure hunter, then you just have a dusting fetish. Thanks for dusting the library for me."

"You're welcome, I'm sure."

"Care to tell me what you were actually doing in there?"

"All right, I guess I owe you that much," she sighed. "I run the local library. We're hoping to add a small museum to it. I'm also an historian; I want to write the history of Higgston. I was hoping to find some references in that library to help me."

"And maybe find a display piece or two."

"Busted," she nodded. "The place has been abandoned for years; I didn't see the harm in it."

"Understood. I won't make a fuss about this, Mara. You didn't do any harm. It's starting to get dark; do you want a ride home?"

"It's not far, but thank you."

"Can you tell me what you meant about treasure?"

"There was supposed to be a treasure hidden in the mansion by the Miller's grandfather. There were always people coming around trying to get into the place, but the old caretaker had a shotgun. He died a couple of years ago, so now I guess they think it's fair game."

"Aw crap, that's just what I need; a bunch of idiots tearing up the place before I have a chance to go over it."

"Go over it? Are you hunting for the treasure too?"

"Yes and no. I'm looking for a treasure all right, but not the one of legend. You'd better get on the go if you don't want that ride."

Mara nodded then fled around the corner of the house. Jace watched her go, enjoying the view until she disappeared down the hill. "Well, what do you know? The old place held both a damsel and a dragon. The dragon is an unknown factor, but the damsel was a pure delight. I wonder what her story is."

He shook his head and walked back into the dark old house. Once again an angry presence tried to block his path. "Bugger off, Gramps. You're not going to scare me out of this."

The lights didn't work and neither did the plumbing, so Jace abandoned the idea of staying there overnight. He headed for a motel he'd seen on his way into town and vowed to investigate the caretaker's cottage first thing in the morning.

MORNING FOUND JACE back at the cottage. It was clear that it needed cleaning and some work, but the plumbing was working. He took his time, closely inspecting everything. He doubted that anything would have been hidden there, but he took no chances. The day was nearly gone when he returned to the motel.

The next morning saw a different Jace Harper. He was clean shaven and wearing a suit. Stopping at town hall he paid the back taxes and arranged to have everything put in his name. Once all the paperwork was in order he took a few brochures from the rack and left. Then he went to the power company and arranged to have the electricity turned on.

Jace stopped in at the diner for a quick lunch. There was a group of women at one of the tables; Mara O'Grady was one of them. They were laughing and enjoying themselves as well as stealing glances at him. He grinned slightly to himself and ignored them.

Having finished his meal, Jace rose and spoke softly to the tiny waitress as he paid his bill. Suddenly he turned quickly to the women, winked at Mara, and then strode through the door. Mara blushed deeply and there was a round of giggles at her expense as Jace disappeared from the room.

Walking back to his car, Jace grinned to himself. That had been a sweet bit of fun. Jace Harper was a man who had denied himself everything all young men revel in. He had done it to dig himself out of debt before it crushed him. There'd been no time for love, only work, but he had signed away his right to work. Come riches or poverty, he was retired. Now there was nothing left but time.

"Ah hell," he sighed. "Not just yet. I still have a bit of work left to do before I relax." Pushing thoughts of Mara O'Grady aside, he looked at the Higgston business directory. A couple of calls later he had a full cleaning crew at the cottage. By the time darkness fell, the place was spotless, all the furniture had been removed by the charity folks, and he was sitting on the floor eating a pizza.

He camped there for several days before his own furniture arrived and the power was hooked up. He spent those days carefully searching the house for the clue and map fragment. Jace was meticulous and had barely managed to satisfy himself that two of the bedrooms were clear. Overwhelm and despair began to set in. This seemed hopeless.

To completely complicate matters, he couldn't seem to get Mara O'Grady out of his thoughts. Something would have to be done about that; he needed to focus. With a heavy sigh, Jace beat the dust from his jeans and headed back to the cottage. As soon as he was outside the door in the fresh air the gloom began to lift.

Jace caught himself and turned to face the house. "So that's the way it's going to be, is it? You're working against me too? If you keep this up I'll have to take steps." He turned and walked back to the cottage. He didn't want to go that route. His mother had been locked in a mental institution for years and subjected to shock treatments for traveling that road.

From Trespasser to...?

Mara reached home and raced to the bathroom. She relieved herself, then climbed into the shower to wash away the dust from the day. What a strange day it had been. Her first adventure into tomb raiding hadn't gone all that well. She'd been busted by the new owner and sent packing. She'd come up empty.

"Mara O'Grady," she admonished herself, "just what the hell possessed you to dust the library. You went there to search for information, not to play housemaid." She actually blushed slightly as she recalled the grin on Jace's face as he thanked her for dusting the books. Mara's cheeks flushed again as she recalled how he had looked her over and the thrill that had sent through her.

"Oh stop it, Mara," she admonished herself, as she toweled herself off then slipped on a fuzzy robe and padded to the kitchen. "You're not fifteen years old having a hormone rush because a high school senior spoke to you; you're a grown woman and well past all that." It did her no good at all for she couldn't get that thrill out of her mind. For the first time in years a man had looked at her as a desirable woman and she'd enjoyed it.

"He sure is cute, though," she giggled, as she sat to a meal of leftovers warmed in the microwave. "Stop it. Now review what happened. What actually went on today?

"Well, I got there but had to go to the back door. There was a presence there that tried to make me run away. There was another one too that seemed to want me to stay."

As a child Mara had talked to spirits but had been vigorously discouraged. It's not real, Mara; it's just pretend in your mind. Mara hadn't actually stopped; she just stopped telling people about it.

"That was a fifty-fifty so I went in anyway," she continued, as she processed the day in her mind. "I poked around until I found the library. Oh gods, what a library. I'd kill to add that to the town's collection. Anyway, that's where I seemed to lose control. I just couldn't help myself; I had to clean it up, to care for it.

"Hmmm, the unfriendly really wanted me out of there, but the other didn't. I think somebody held me there for some reason. Anyway, that's where I got busted by Jace Harper. He was actually pretty sweet about it. I could have been arrested.

"I wonder if he likes to dance..."

By the next day Jace was the talk of the town. Somebody had claimed the Miller Mansion. Stories ranged from him wanting to tear it down and burn it to wanting to open it as a B&B. Others said he was a land developer who was going to make a sub-division there. Mara just listened politely and kept her opinions to herself. In truth she had no idea what he was planning to do with the old place.

At lunch she endured the third degree from her sister and friends. Had she gone up to the Miller place? Did she find anything? Not really. Did she get busted by the new owner? Yes. What's he look like? What's his voice like? Is he cute? Is he single? It went on and on until they all knew everything, including how he'd looked her over, but she wouldn't say how she'd felt about that. They teased her anyway.

The next day he showed up at the diner for lunch. The girls were at their favorite table, chatting away as he came in. They fell silent as he spoke a single word and smiled. "Ladies." He then went to a booth and sat. He didn't look up even once as he ate, but how could he not know he was the topic of conversation? Mara blushed and blushed again as she tried to shush her friends.

Jace paid for his meal then winked at her on his way out. She blushed again as the teasing reached new levels. A few minutes later they learned he'd paid for their meal too.

That night Mara dreamed of Jace Harper. It was an extremely erotic dream and she awakened fully aroused. She let her agile fingers dance across her body until a shattering orgasm washed over her and she returned to sleep. This time in her dream, he just held her gently.

A number of days went by without a glimpse of him, yet he still filled her thoughts. He'd said he too was looking for treasure, but not that kind. What had he meant? What was he looking for? It was really none of her business, but Mara was curious. She had her starting point for her historical research. She'd research everything she could about the old run down place on the hill.

There was usually a lull in the early afternoon, so she left Louise on duty and headed for the archives. It took a bit of searching, but Mara found the original plans for the Miller place. She pored over them for hours, trying to see what was hidden. About the same time Jace was ready to give up, Mara made her discovery. She determined to share the knowledge with Jace at first opportunity.

It had been a couple of months since Jace had bought the girls lunch and he had rarely been seen about the town since. Mara was standing with her back to the library door when she heard the soft jingle of the bell. She turned to find Jace Harper smiling at her. His eyes were roaming over her figure and she blushed again with delight. Dammit, she had to stop that foolishness.

"Hello, Mr. Harper," she smiled, as she put down the book that she'd had in her hand. "Is it true you've been asking about me around town? Is there some information you need?" She grinned with delight to see him slightly discomfited. She'd won that round.

Finally he shook off the spell and gave her a rueful grin. "Yes, I've been checking you out," he admitted. "Can I talk to you in private?"

"We're alone here for the moment," she replied, as she indicated a chair by her desk. She walked behind the desk and sat gracefully. "What's on your mind? Are you going to have me arrested?"

"Well, I suppose I should," he grinned as he sat facing her. "It's not safe to leave a cat burglar loose in the town. Alas, that's not why I've come. I checked you out and everybody says you're a highly intelligent and trustworthy woman. I've come to offer a bargain."

"A bargain? Mr. Harper, just what are you up to?"

"Jace, please, Mara. Please read this." He pushed a folder across the desk to her.

"What is this, Jace?"

"That is a transcript of my grandfather's last will and testament."

"I don't understand."

"Read it and I think you will."

Bemused, Mara opened the file and, pushing her glasses back into place, she began to read. A moment later her jaw dropped and her mouth formed a perfect O. Jace had to look away to keep from leaping across the desk to kiss that perfect mouth.

"Oh my dear lord," she said, as she continued reading. "Why that misbegotten son of a Siberian sea cook. What a vile, contemptible old man. Oops, sorry. I didn't mean to speak ill of your grandfather."

"Go ahead," sighed Jace. "I curse the old goat soundly every day, the evil old son of a..."

"This is unbelievable," declared Mara, as she closed the file. "Are all five of you involved?"

"Yes, it was all or nothing. We considered fighting the will, but by then we had willingly signed our lives away. Round one goes to Gramps. I checked in with the others briefly last night. None of us has found anything. Round two goes to Gramps."

"So, why have you come to me with this?"

"I need help. Everyone in town says you're the smartest person they've ever met, that you're completely honest and discrete, that you have a keen interest in history, and that you have the luck of the Irish. I need someone with all those traits to help me solve this puzzle.

"Mara, I know you covet that library, and you can have it once we're convinced it doesn't contain the prize. Help me and I'll give you the damn thing. If we crack it and get the pot of gold at the end of the rainbow, I'll turn that house into a library/museum for you."

Mara took a moment to process what he had just said. She was having trouble staying focused on his words instead of the nearness of him. "You're serious?"

"Deadly serious. I'm completely out of my depth here. I need you."

She blinked her eyes and looked away. How many times in her life had she longed to hear a man say just those words and mean them? Too many, and this man was sincere. Sadly he needed her for the wrong reason. "*Dammit, Mara, not now,*" she thought, "*this is not the time or place for this. Get a grip and stop being so damn needy.*"

Mara drew a deep breath then nodded. "All right, Jace, I'll do what I can. It'll have to be on my days off as I can't leave my job."

"I understand," he replied, relief clear in his voice. "Can we start Saturday morning?"

"Yes, of course," she replied, as they both rose to their feet.

"Mara, you have to keep this completely secret; at least until we've got what we're after."

"I understand," she replied. "Mum's the word."

"Great," he smiled, as he stood and offered his hand to seal the deal. "See you bright and early Saturday."

"I'll be there," she smiled, as she clasped the offered hand. "*Until we get what we want; I wonder, Jace Harper, do you have any idea what I really want? Do I, for that matter?*"

"WAS THAT THE NEW OWNER of the Miller place just leaving?" asked Louise as she came in for her afternoon shift.

"Indeed it was."

"So, is he suing you? Or having you arrested?"

"Neither," laughed Mara. "He wants me to have a look at the old library. He's thinking he might donate some or all of it. He wants me to see if anything is worth salvaging."

"Oh really? Do you think there might be something worthwhile up there?"

"There well may be," Mara replied saucily, as she swept her sweater across her shoulders and headed for the door.

"Enjoy your lunch," smiled Louise, as Mara disappeared through the door. Louise turned to the task of restocking books on the shelves. She hummed happily to herself as she worked. Things were moving along perfectly. Mara shouldn't be alone, and this man seemed to have caught her interest.

Saturday morning arrived and Mara, dressed in tight jeans and a top that hugged her curves, set out for the old Miller place. She was wearing make-up, something she rarely ever did. She fussed and debated with herself for an hour, calling herself a foolish school girl, but she'd done it anyway. Jace met her at the door and the look on his face told her it had been the right decision.

Opening the Library

Jace Harper knew he needed help. Being able to admit that and accept it had always been one of his strong suits. Another was his ability to choose the right person for the job. This time he had a strong hunch it was Mara O'Grady he needed. A few inquiries about the town convinced him of it. He gathered up his information and went to see her at the library.

She was standing back to him as he entered, and he paused to drink the sight of her. What was it about this woman that drew him so? Fighting his hormones and rising lust, he shook off the spell and responded to her greeting. It was time for the sales pitch.

Once Mara agreed to help him, Jace set to work. He had the power turned on to the big house and the water hooked up again. By the time Friday night rolled around, he was as ready for her as he could be. He'd cut and cleaned a path to the front door, managed to get one powder room working, and a path to the library, as well as the room itself cleaned.

"What the hell is it about this woman," he sighed, as he lay back on his bed late Friday evening. "I can't seem to get her out of my mind. The sound of her voice, her laughter, and those eyes, oh god, those eyes. Cripes, if she had any idea at all of what she does to me I'd be doomed. Hell, if she had any idea of the lust she creates in me, she'd run for the hills. Dammit all anyway, this is really going to complicate things."

Saturday morning arrived and a freshly groomed Jace met Mara at the door. His jaw dropped as he got a clear look at her. She blushed softly as she noticed his expression. Trying desperately to hide the fact he was flustered; he greeted her and opened the door wide. "Good morning, Mara. You're looking lovely this morning."

"Why thank you, Jace. You hired a cleaning crew? This place looks spotless."

"I hired a crew for the cottage only," he replied, as he led her to the library. "I did this myself. We have a safe path to the library and a working powder room right adjacent to it. The rest of the house is a disaster."

"Forgive me," she smiled, as she hung her sweater on the back of a chair and set her bag on the long table. "I half expected to see the place torn apart."

"That was my first thought, but I held back," he chuckled. "Gramps was a devious old bugger. He was also a schemer. I don't believe he hid anything in a conventional way. I expect tearing the place apart to find the clue would be the worst thing we could do. No, I'm convinced the clue is in this room somewhere."

"All right, where would you like to begin?"

"That, my dear, is entirely up to you," he sighed. "What do you suggest?"

Mara thought for a moment. "I think we should start on the second floor," she replied. "First we search a small area, disturbing nothing. Then we empty all the books from a single shelf and inspect both the shelf and each book minutely. Does that make sense?"

"You're the boss. Where do you want to start?"

"Follow me." She smiled as she headed for the stairs. He was more than happy to do so. She could feel his eyes on her as he followed her up the steps and she shivered with delight. *"Focus, Mara, focus,"* she silently admonished herself.

The second level of the library was a wide mezzanine. Bookcases loaded with volumes lined the walls and two long tables with chairs were there for reading. "Let's start here," she said, as she reached the corner farthest from the stairs. "First we check this wall then, one by one, empty and clear the bookcases."

"I checked these walls when I was cleaning," he replied. "I didn't find anything."

"Very well, then, let's begin with this bookcase. Help me pile all the books on this table then I'll start on the books while you check the case and the wall behind it. Oh, check the floor under it as well."

"Yes ma'am," he grinned, as they set to work.

They carefully piled all the books from the shelf on one end of the table. While Jace pulled the case out from the wall and began his inspection, Mara took a large notepad and pen from her bag. She sat and reached for the first book. Jace stopped to watch.

Mara held the first book open and fanned the pages; nothing fell out so she fanned them more carefully and found a pressed flower. She noted the find, the name of the book and the page she'd discovered it, and then turned her attention to the binding.

The binding was inspected carefully; it yielded nothing. She then carefully ran her fingertips over every inch of the book's leather cover. Satisfied it held no further secrets; Mara set it at the opposite end of the table and reached for another. With a grin of delight, Jace returned to his own task.

When Jace was satisfied the bookcase held no secrets he turned his attention to the wall and floor. Coming up empty, he replaced the bookcase against the wall. He sat facing Mara and reached for a book. She carefully explained what to look for and he set to work. By mid-afternoon they had a few small finds laid aside and cataloged.

Jace stretched and rose from the chair. "I'm half starved," he announced. "Shall I go for some pizza or something?"

"I brought us a picnic lunch," she smiled, as she too leaned back to rub the knots out of her neck and shoulders. She stood and stretched. "First a pee break then we eat."

"Works for me," he smiled. "Ladies first; powder room is downstairs, a left and follow the stacks around. You can't miss it." She smiled her thanks and danced down the circular staircase. When she returned she found that he'd re-stacked all the books they had cleared. When he returned from the washroom he found she had re-arranged the books on the shelf.

"I messed it up, huh?"

"Just a bit," she smiled. "I'm sorry, Jace, but I am a librarian."

"It would drive you crazy?"

"Stark raving mad," she grinned.

"Can't have that," he laughed. "You mentioned food."

"Oh yes, here." She took ham and cheese sandwiches from the bag, a container of fresh fruit slices, and a thermos of coffee. "I'm sorry; the coffee has cream and sugar. I didn't know how you like yours."

"Perfect," he smiled, as he sat and reached for a sandwich. She poured the coffee into two mugs she'd brought.

"May I ask, Mara; what are those lists you've made?"

"Sure. This is the list of what we found and where we found it. This notepad has a list of the books I've inspected and would like to keep, this list is of damaged or moldy books, and this is a small list of rare books. There are some truly wonderful treasures here. Mr. Miller was a real collector."

Mara removed and polished her glasses on her shirt tail then replaced them on her face. She could see him smiling at her. "What?"

"You're really passionate about books, aren't you?"

"Yes, I am," she replied. "What are you passionate about?"

"I don't know," he replied with slumping shoulders. "This was supposed to be my year to find out, but this madness came along and screwed that up."

"Oh? Care to share?"

"Not really."

"Sorry," she replied, averting her eyes, "I didn't mean to pry."

"Mara, I'm the only child of a drunken fool. My father drank us into poverty and debt then killed himself and my mother by crashing his car into a concrete wall. The insurance company wouldn't pay, and I was twenty-two years old with a combined student debt and family debt of well over six figures. I worked my ass off day and night to get out of debt. That happened three months ago.

"This was supposed to be my year to play and find myself. You already know how that went sideways. So, how did you become a librarian?"

"I lived my life in books from the moment I learned to read," she sighed. "I studied History and Library Science, got my degree, came back home, established a small library, and began my quest to write the history of Higgston."

"When did you take up burglary?"

"Oh, that's new," she replied, her silvery laughter dancing off the walls and sending thrills through him. "You know, Grandma's trust fund isn't what it used to be with inflation and all. I needed a second job, and with no other marketable skills, well..."

"So, this was your first heist?"

"Yes, it was my first day on the job. Guess I should have gone in for more training."

"Actually, I think sleuthing is a career more suited to your talents," he grinned. "You certainly seem to have the skills for it."

"Why thank you, kind sir. Does that mean it's time to get back to work?"

"Yep," he replied, as he handed her a book and chose one for himself. When he finished his inspection of the book he passed it to her and she gave it a quick inspection, added it to one of her lists then passed him another.

They finished the pile of books then turned their attention to the few treasures they'd found. Using Mara's notes, they retrieved the book from whence came the pressed flower. Returning to the page they noted the stain from the pressing, but there were no markings, nothing was highlighted, nothing outstanding about the placement at all, so they dismissed the flower.

The same procedure was repeated for the bookmark, the dollar bill, and the two folded receipts. By the time they finished it was growing dark outside. Jace walked Mara to the gate. He offered to walk her home, but she refused saying it wasn't far and she was familiar with the town. With a smile and a cheerful, "See you tomorrow," she was gone down the hill. Jace watched her retreating form until she was out of sight.

During the day the two spirits that haunted the place had been evident. The one had tried to drive them away, but the other had been there to give them hope. Also, when they were both in the same room the hopeful spirit seemed to be stronger. As Jace walked back inside alone a wave of depression and fear fell upon him.

"Give it up, Gramps," he growled. "I'm not leaving and there's not a damned thing you can do about it. I've spent the day with Mara O'Grady. Life is good." With a smile on his face Jace locked up the house and retreated to the cottage for a meal, a shower, and a good night's sleep.

Mara smiled to herself as she put a bit more action in her walk. She knew he was watching, and she wanted to give him a show. Inside her head her board of directors, as she called it, was in hot debate. Her desires, longings, experiences, and conscience all battled for her attention. Desire and longing had teamed up and were winning.

She reached home and showered before making herself a small meal. She sat in the living room to eat but didn't turn on the television or open a book. Her thoughts were solely on Jace Harper. Mara had no idea why this man held her attention like no other ever had.

Giving her imagination free reign, she pictured him here beside her. She saw his tall rangy build, a bit soft from years of riding a desk, but lean and growing hard from all the work around the old run down place. His hair, not quite brown and not quite red, was beginning to grow out a bit and curl up around his neck. She had fought the urge to run her fingers through those curls all day.

Mara wasn't sure which she found the most attractive, his eyes or his mouth. His eyes were not quite green and not quite blue but could be either depending on the light. They seemed to grow dark, almost brown, when he concentrated.

His mouth, however, fascinated her. His lips at rest had almost a cruel twist to them and that deepened as his mood grew more frustrated or if he focused hard. That look vanished the instant he smiled and lit up her world. Mara blushed at how badly she wanted him to crush that mouth against her own, hungry for her, claiming her.

"Stop it, Mara," she admonished herself aloud. She rose and returned to the kitchen, depositing the dishes in the sink. "You've been here before and look where it got you."

"No you haven't," whispered a soft voice from the edges of her reality, "not here. This is something more than you have ever experienced before or will again. Release yourself to it, Mara."

Mara stopped still; her face ashen. She hadn't heard that voice for a long time, and hoped to never hear it again, for another, evil voice always seemed to accompany it. "So, you're back," she said aloud. "Go away and leave me alone. I have no desire to spend the rest of my life in an institution on happy drugs."

"A bargain then," replied the faint voice. "Allow yourself to enjoy this man and I won't return unless you call for me."

"Deal," said Mara, and then looked around guiltily, hoping no one had heard her talking to herself. Mara let her shoulders sag as she walked to her bathroom and opened the medicine chest. She took down the medicine bottle and gazed at it for a long time then put it back, unopened.

"Not this time," she muttered, as she returned to the living room. "I've had enough of that crap. I'm older and stronger now. I can handle this." Mara had spent far too much of her adolescence in therapy and taking drugs that made her mind fuzzy. Telling her parents that she heard voices had been a huge mistake. This time she planned to face it head on.

"I have to call Meghan," she muttered, as she reached for the phone and hit the speed dial.

"Hey, Sis," came Meghan's cheerful voice, "what's up? How did your date with Jace Harper go?"

"Meg, I've got a problem."

"Oh honey, we just have to do your hair a bit..."

"Meghan, shut up, just listen. Meg, they're back."

"Oh shit," breathed Meghan. "Honey, have you got any meds on hand? Do you need me to come over?"

"Easy, girl. Yes, I have meds, but didn't take any. Not yet, I'm not going there unless I absolutely have to."

"All right, sister, talk to me."

"It was just the friendly. She encouraged me to continue to indulge my fantasies about Jace. I got nasty and she agreed to go away as long as I let myself fall for Jace Harper."

"You're serious?"

"I am."

"So, is that going to be a hard thing?"

"Hell no," sighed Mara, as she sank deeper into her chair. "It'll be all too damned easy. I'm probably going to get my heart broken here, but I want to see if the voice will keep the bargain. If it does, then I know the voices were always real and not my imagination or a brain imbalance or anything. I'll know I'm not crazy. That alone will be worth the heartbreak."

"Wow. Gods, Mara, you're so brave and strong. What do you need me to do?"

"Keep an eye on me like always, but don't let me go chasing Jace Harper all over town either. It'll be one thing to fall for the guy; that's the easy part, but I don't want to run around all over town like a teenage stalker making wedding plans. If he actually likes and wants me he's going to have to come to me."

"Oh god, Mara," laughed Meghan, "you're so fierce. You inspire me, big sister. All right; I'll be your watch dog. Just remember, when I get in your face or mess things up with Jace Harper, this was your idea."

"Thanks, Meg, I think," sighed Mara. "See you at coffee Monday?"

"Sure, but what are you up to tomorrow?"

"Same thing I'll be doing every weekend for the next few months; hanging out in Jace Harper's library."

"Don't do anything I wouldn't do," laughed Meghan.

"That gives me way too much leeway," chuckled Mara. "See you Monday."

"Night, Sis, have naughty dreams."

While Mara wrestled with her demons, Jace encountered one of his own. He'd gone home, showered, and warmed up a frozen dinner. Finding himself hungry he had another. Sitting sprawled on his easy chair he let his thoughts return to Mara O'Grady. What was it about this woman? At first glance she would seem quite plain, but a second look put the lie to that. Mara was striking with that dark hair and pale skin with flashing brown eyes.

To top it off, she was smart, and Jace liked intelligent women. From their conversations this day he knew he would spend a lifetime with her trying to keep up intellectually. The girl fascinated him on every level.

He tried to form a mental picture of her sitting in the room with him and it was far easier than he might have thought. He could see her reading, her eyes eagerly following the story as her graceful fingers flicked the pages.

"Well, Jace old buddy, there surely is one treasure here in Higgston," he sighed aloud. "The real trick will be to claim her."

Distracted

Jace went to sleep with thoughts of Mara O'Grady, hoping to dream of her. It didn't happen. Instead, his dreams were invaded by strange adventures and an awareness of a brooding sense of doom.

In the dream, Jace watched as time slipped back several centuries. He saw a poor man standing before a rustic cabin. A tall, angry man faced him, a flint-lock pistol in his hand. "Where is she, Elijah Merryman?" he demanded.

"Gone," replied the poor man.

"I'll find her, you know. I'll find her and have justice for my losses."

"That you will not, Phidias Tomlinson. You're a fool and I'll denounce you before the council of elders. Your wealth will not protect you from the lies you've told."

The pistol fired in a puff of smoke and Jace felt the impact as the lead ball struck. A stomach wound. The man would take a long time to die. "Find her," roared the gunman, "get on the trail and find her. Bring the witch to me; she will face the death she deserves." He stalked away and climbed back into the buggy he had driven to the small farm. Whipping up the horse, he sped away.

Jace tossed and turned, feeling the pain and despair of the wounded man. As life passed into mystery, a woman appeared and knelt beside the dead man, tears of anguish and loss streaming down her face. With a snarl of rage she took up some of her husband's spilled blood and drew five symbols on the ground.

"You've done this, Phidias Tomlinson, and I curse you for it. By the power of his spilled blood and that of my own, I curse you, and all who spring from you, with madness until the time no male children fall from your line. Wealth is your god and you shall have it, but madness will be its bride, and so will it be for all male children in your line until the line is broken and your evil revealed for all to see."

Jace cried out in horror as she drove a knife into her own body and, with her dying breath she repeated the symbols with the blood that poured from the wound. He tried to drive away the vision, but he failed.

As Jace struggled to escape the dream, another woman appeared and found the bodies. She screamed a vain protest and fell across them, weeping. She looked so distraught, Jace wanted to comfort her, and then her eyes changed as the rage built in her. "I see what you have done, my sister."

She pulled the knife from her sister's breast and cut open her own palm. "By all the power I wield, I add my pledge to this curse. My line will see it done." She held her clenched fist over each symbol and squeezed some of her own blood onto the markings. And then Jace awakened, soaked in sweat.

Shaken to his core, he lay breathing shallowly, trying to clear his head. "A dream," he sighed deeply then shuddered as he drew another deep breath. "It was only a dream."

"No dream, Jace Harper," whispered a voice from the edges of his reality, "but the truth of your beginnings. The time has come to purge the spirit of Phidias Tomlinson from this world. He has inhabited all his descendants until now, driving them to madness and greed. We blocked him with your grandfather so the male line is broken. You must now defeat him, discover his greatest secret, and then bring it to light."

"Great, now I'm hearing voices," he growled, as he rose and padded to the bathroom. He relieved himself then returned to the kitchen, too awake for sleep now. 5:45 A.M... Jace put on a pot of coffee and sat to the table to wait until it was ready. He tried to invoke the voice again, but the only answer was his practical side.

"Write it all down. Tell Mara." Jace grabbed a pen and notebook and wrote it all down as he remembered it.

While Jace wrestled with the nightmare, Mara was having a dream of a different sort. In her dream she and Jace were locked in a passionate embrace. She felt the heat of his body, his desire, his driving need for her in every thrust. She rose up to meet each one, aching, wanting, devouring his need and feeding it with her own. Her arms and legs encircled him, drawing him closer, tighter, as though to absorb him completely, drowning in the sensations, and demanding more.

Mara awakened with a scream of pleasure, orgasming in her bed as she orgasmed in the dream. She lay gasping in her soaked sheets, drawing precious air deep into her lungs. "Oh my dear sweet god," she breathed, as she began to return to her senses, "one day I hope to actually have sex half that good." With a sweet smile of satiation, she drifted off to sleep again.

"GOOD MORNING, JACE," sang Mara, as she stepped past him and into the house. "I've brought us a thermos of coffee and a snack for later. Did you sleep well?"

"Not a bit," he sighed, as he allowed her bright cheer lift his spirits. "I had a horrifying nightmare."

"Oh, I'm sorry to hear that." Mara draped her sweater across the back of a chair and began to gather books from the second bookshelf.

Jace helped her clear off the case, then slid it out to inspect behind it. "Yes, it was scary stuff; gave me the creeps. I wrote it down because I want to ask you about some of it."

"Oh?" she said, glancing up as she lowered herself gracefully into the chair.

"It seemed too real to be a dream," he replied, as he straightened up and turned to face her. "I'm wondering if it was something old Gramps sent to give me the creeps and chase me away." He finished his inspection and, finding nothing of interest, circled the table and sat facing her as he had the day before.

"That's possible, I guess. You said you wrote it down; may I see it?"

"I was hoping you'd ask." He grinned as he took a folded paper from his pocket and passed it to her. Mara smoothed out the paper and read it, her face becoming serious, then drifting into puzzled thoughtfulness. "Mara?"

"That name seems familiar somehow, something about history. May I keep this? I'd like to poke around the library this week and see if I can discover anything about these names. Perhaps this wasn't Gramps trying to creep you out, but something else."

"That's what I was afraid of," he sighed, as he began to inspect a book.

"Jace, what haven't you told me?"

"You'll just think I'm crazy. I don't want to be locked up in a rubber room."

Mara laughed at that, her silvery voice lingering in the air and driving the gloom from his heart. Jace thought he would do anything at all to make her laugh. "Now why would I think you're crazy, Mr. Harper?" Seeing his face and the way he was avoiding eye contact made her turn serious again. "Jace, I promise you I'll take very seriously whatever you tell me about this."

Jace sighed and brought his eyes back to meet hers as she reached across the table to grip his hand. "All right, Mara, but I'll hold you to that. The damned nightmare woke me up. I got up to fix a snack and clear my head. That's when I heard it."

"Heard what?"

"The voice, a woman's voice, very soft, like she was far away."

"What did she say to you?" Mara's eye's bored into his intently and Jace started to get lost in those eyes again. He shook it off and responded.

"She said it was the truth of my beginnings. She said it was time to purge the spirit of Phidias Tomlinson forever. He's inhabited all his descendants until now, driving them to madness and greed. She said that ended with Gramps. She said I had to defeat him, discover his greatest secret, and then bring it to light.

"Mara, I'm not crazy and I didn't just imagine that part. It was real."

"I believe you, Jace. I do believe you."

"Oh really? Just like that?"

"Yes, just like that. Jace, I've heard that voice, and another, all my life. I made the mistake of confiding in my parents and spent many years on meds as a result. I finally began to lie to the shrinks, telling them I could no longer hear the voice. After a while I couldn't hear it anymore and thought that part of my life was finally over. A few days ago the voice came back."

"What did it say?" Jace's voice was choked, barely audible.

"It told me to help you with your quest."

There was a soft blush at her cheek and Jace wondered what else the voice had said, but he let it go. "All right," he declared, as he regained his voice. "Let's proceed as though we're both completely sane. If we hear from the voice and want to discuss it, we have to be in private."

"Agreed," she replied, her bright smile back in place and dazzling him once again. "We mustn't let the mortals know we have special powers."

"Indeed not," he grinned, getting lost in her eyes once again.

The day passed slowly and pleasantly with a lot of stolen glances between them. "That's the last one," sighed Mara, as she rubbed the back of her neck.

"Another dud," grumbled Jace.

"Don't be so impatient," laughed Mara. "We've just completely eliminated another section. We'll keep going until we find it. If it isn't in the library then we'll approach the rest of the house the same way. Jace, we will find it."

"Thanks for the pep talk, Mara," he grinned. "It worked. So, can I buy you a meal at the diner if it's open?"

"Oh, it's open for a few more hours. My friend owns the place, and she says you can't make money with the door shut."

"Let's go then," he said, as he rose to his feet.

"We have to re-stock the shelves first," she admonished with mock severity.

"Of course we do. What the hell was I thinking?" that made her laugh and again that sweet laughter lifted his spirits. "You can leave your lists there if you want, Mara."

"Thanks, but I want to go over them; compare them to the town's lists. I know we didn't find your treasure, Jace, but we sure found treasure. Some of these books are quite rare and in excellent shape. You really should have some sort of security set up here."

"You're right about that," he said, as he followed her down the stairs. "I'll see what I can do this week. What do you think; bright lights and cameras?"

"Yes, and modern locks too."

They walked to the café, Jace quizzing her about certain landmarks and Mara giving him some of the history of Higgston. They entered and chose a booth by the window. The tall red-haired waitress appeared and set a cup of coffee at Mara's elbow. It already had cream and sugar in it. "She's got to be Mara's sister," thought Jace, as he noted the family resemblance.

"Jace," smiled Mara, "this is my sister, Meghan. Meg, this is Jace Harper."

"Hi, welcome to Higgston," smiled Meghan, as she lightly gripped then released his hand.

"Thanks."

"So, how are you enjoying our little town?" Meghan set the second cup of pre-mixed coffee at his place.

With a quirked eyebrow, Jace tasted it. Perfect. "Tell me, Meghan, how did you know how I like my coffee?"

"I'm an Irish witch and I know many things I'm not supposed to," she grinned, then she relented. "I heard you order it the other week."

"Ah ha, okay, in answer to your question, I'm enjoying Higgston. There are some lovely views here."

"I'm sure there are," she replied as she nudged Mara gently. "I warn you, Jace Harper, flattery will get you everywhere around here."

"Now that is good to know," he grinned.

"Stop it, both of you," said Mara. "You promised to feed me."

"And so, to work," laughed Meghan. "What'll it be, folks?"

"The big burger and whatever soup you've got on the go," replied Mara.

"Jace?"

"Works for me."

"Be back in a jiffy," she sang, as she turned away with light steps. Mara blushed softly and her heart sang to note Jace's eyes didn't follow Meghan's tall lithe figure, but remained on her as her sexy sister walked away.

They drank their coffee in a comfortable silence, each just enjoying the nearness of the other. "There's something else I'd like to talk to you about," said Jace, as he set his empty coffee cup back on the table.

"Oh?"

"Yes. It's time for the first meeting of the minds. My cousins and I decided to hold off on the first of our monthly meetings for a couple of months. You know, to give us all time to get settled in. However, the time has come. The boys will be in town next week, Thursday and Friday. I'd like for you to meet them."

"I'd love to."

"Boys? What's all this about meeting boys?" grinned Meghan, as she scooted into the booth beside Mara. "If there are boys coming, I want to meet them too."

"Forgive me, Mara," smiled Jace. "I had no idea your sister was so shy."

"Meg? Shy?" laughed Mara. "That'll be the day. Go on Meg, get out and bring me some food." She playfully pushed her sister from the booth, and with a mischievous smile, Meghan headed for the kitchen. Again Jace Harper's eyes remained on Mara. "God, she was always such a brat."

"She seems like a lot of fun, Mara. I think you're secretly quite proud of her."

"I am. No matter how depressed I might get, Meg always pulls me up out of it. She's always been the one I could count on the most.

"Now, tell me why you want me to meet the guys."

"I want to show them I've already found the treasure of Higgston."

"Give that up, Jace Harper," she smiled. "You might turn Meghan's head with that flattery, but I want the truth from you."

"All right," he grinned, "but I meant what I said. Mara, your insights to the workings of this quest will be invaluable, not just to me, but to all of us. Remember, all five of us have to succeed or nobody succeeds. Besides, you're my partner in the quest for treasure; you need to be at the meetings."

"Thank you for the compliment, Jace. Yes, I agree, and I would love to sit in on the meetings. I confess I find the whole thing quite exciting."

"Oh, so now we're at the exciting part," smiled Meghan, as she set the food on the table. "What's so exciting?"

"Meghan O'Grady," Jace sighed elaborately, "if I promise to introduce you to the guys, will you give us a few minute's peace?"

"It's a deal," she grinned. "Let me know when you're finished or if you need anything. Hang on to this one, Mara. I like him; he has a sense of humor." With that she stepped away, leaving them alone to enjoy their meal and each other.

The Meeting

The energy between them got a bit awkward when he walked her back to her apartment building. It was as though both had slipped back into those teenage years when the first date was over and neither quite knew how to make it end right. They stood at the door, he wanting desperately to pull her close and kiss her, and she wanting him to do it. They didn't get the chance.

"Ah, Mara, just the woman I wanted to see," said a big man in coveralls, as he spotted them at the door. "I've got time to fix that leaky faucet for you now, if you'd like."

The mood broken, Mara shook of the spell and turned to the building manager. "That'd be great," she said. "I'll be right up."

She turned back to Jace and took his hands. "Thanks for treating me to dinner."

"All my pleasure," he smiled, as he too, shook off the spell of desire. "Again next Wednesday? We should go over our notes before the guys get here."

"Sure," she replied. "Pick me up at six?"

"Perfect," he replied. He gave her hands a gentle squeeze and she responded in kind.

"Some time tonight, Mara," bellowed a male voice from inside.

"Coming," she called in reply. "Good night, Jace. See you Wednesday."

"Wednesday," he replied, as her fingers slipped from his grasp and she stepped through the door.

"I don't think I like that guy much," grumbled Jace, as he turned his footsteps towards home.

Jace was still lost in thoughts of Mara and sweet daydreams of what her kiss would be like when he realized he'd returned to the house, not the cottage. A swift movement at the library window brought him back to Earth in a hurry. Dammit, he'd forgotten to lock the door. Watching carefully, he approached and opened the door slowly. "I know you're in here and I have a gun," he called, as he threw on the hallway lights.

The shadow of a large man raced from the library door and out through the back of the house. Jace leaped after him, but the man was well away before Jace cleared the house. "Dammit," he swore, and turned on all the lights and began a full inspection of the house. "Mara's right, I need some protection here. Sadly, I need more exercise too. That's twice that bastard has outrun me easily."

After a long careful inspection Jace concluded nothing had been taken. A number of books had been moved off different shelves on the ground floor, but all were there. He finally gave it up and, leaving all the lights on, headed for the cottage, shower, and bed. He lay still on the cool sheets, imagining Mara there beside him.

He could see her plain as day, smiling up at him, lifting her mouth for a kiss. His heart ached for her, and his body burned with desire. Allowing his imagination to bring her into that kiss, her bare nipples pressed to his chest, Jace groaned with the power of it. Taking the living wood in hand, he gave himself over to the fantasy and the relief he so desperately needed.

The power of it built until his consciousness exploded. As he slowly returned to Earth he drifted off to sleep, vowing to clean up the mess in the morning. That night his dreams were pleasant. He dreamed of Mara.

For her part, Mara spent far more time than she'd like listening to Mr. James complain about poor quality, made in Asia, plumbing fixtures. It took him far longer than she'd expected to get a satisfactory repair. By the time he was done and out the door, Meghan arrived, bottle of wine in hand.

"Tell me absolutely everything," said Meghan, as she tossed her coat across the back of the sofa and headed for the kitchen to find the opener and wine glasses. She was back in a jiffy with the opened bottle and a half glass for each.

"There's nothing to tell," sighed Mara, as she sank into a chair and took a sip of the wine. "Jace walked me home and we were just at the door. I was hoping for a goodnight kiss. I know he wanted to as badly as I did."

"So, no kiss? What the heck happened?"

"Mr. James happened. I've been at him for weeks to fix that damned leaky faucet. With perfect timing, as usual, he showed up and started bellowing for me to hurry just as Jace was working up his courage."

"Well that sucks," giggled Meghan. "So what's the plan?"

"The plan?"

"The plan, girl. You like this guy and you two look so sweet together. Tell me you don't want to hook up."

"I don't want to hook up, Meg. Sadly, I want more than a hook up, a lot more."

"Perfect, so what's the plan?"

"The plan, dear sister, is to play it cool and see where it goes. I've been accused of being needy and clingy for the last time. I've learned to live with my own company and be happy. If a man wants me, he'd better be willing to let it show and mean it."

"Wow, you go, sister. So tell me the rest of it."

"Meg, I don't want halfway ever again. I want it all. I want a man who'll love me, only me, and make that plain. No holding back, no weekends with the boys, and no needing his own space. If I'm going to fall in love I want it all, a full and complete sharing, body, mind, and soul."

"Keep going," smiled Meghan, as she poured more wine for them both.

"I won't push, Meg. I think that may have been the problem before. I wanted it and pushed too hard to make it happen."

"Oh yeah," laughed Meg. "That'll scare the boys away. They're so afraid a woman is trying to trap them, like they're really the important ones. Sorry guys, you should be so lucky. All right, sister of mine, I'm with you. From now on, if a guy wants either of us he'd damn well better let it show and mean it."

They continued to bond and build up each other's confidence until both the evening and the wine were gone. Mara was a bit tipsy when she crawled into bed that night. She giggled as she let her mind run back over the evening.

Jace had said he'd already found Higgston's real treasure. It was a sweet compliment and she loved it. He'd kept his eyes and attention on her all through the meal and the walk home. She'd really wanted to invite him up for a glass of wine and a round of wild sex, but... Perhaps Mr. James' intervention hadn't been all bad. It'd given her time to get some distance on it and think clearly. She never seemed to think clearly when Jace Harper was near.

Still, it would have been delicious to bring him up and seduce him. She'd noticed the way he looked at her and his arousal trying vainly to make room in his jeans. She giggled again as she thought of it. Yes, it truly would have been magic. She let her hands begin to explore her body even as her mind explored the possibilities.

MARA HADN'T SEEN JACE for a couple of days, but had reports from friends that he'd been seen out early, jogging, every morning. That seemed a bit odd, but she let it go, planning to ask him about it on Wednesday.

She left the library early that afternoon. Mara couldn't remember putting this much effort into a date ever before, not really. She bathed and fussed with her hair, painted her nails, then took stock of her wardrobe. There wasn't a lot of sexy in there. She'd gotten rid of it when she crossed thirty and was still single. Hmm.

All right, tight skirt, basic black; push up bra; soft, but snug, blue sweater and heels. Yes, that would do it. Now for the make-up. The heels might be a touch too high, the clothes a bit tight, but Mara wanted this man's attention. She was determined to wait until he declared himself, but she ached for it to happen. He liked looking at her, so she decided there was no harm in giving him something to look at.

He buzzed up and she went down to meet him. Oh dear, this wasn't going to be easy. The man was just too delicious. There he was, smiling at her. Fresh jeans, shiny shoes, dress shirt open at the neck and a blue sport's jacket; it was her favorite look on a man. Either he'd gotten lucky or Meghan had talked out of school. The way he was gaping at her wasn't bad for her ego either.

"Mara, you look stunning." He smiled as she approached. He opened the door of his car and helped her settle in, getting a good look at her legs in the process. "*For the love of god, get a grip, Jace Harper. This is no time for a raging hard-on.*"

"I've booked us a table at the Golden Lookout just out of town."

"Oh, that's supposed to be a really great place. I've never been, but I've heard nice things about it."

"I wanted to take you someplace nice; and I wanted to escape the third degree from your sister," he grinned.

"Good thinking," she laughed. "Wow, this is almost like a date."

"It is a date, Mara," he sighed, as he let his shoulders slump. "At least I want it to be. If you'd rather keep this completely on a professional level tell me now before I make a complete fool of myself."

"I have no objection at all to mixing a bit of pleasure with business," she replied, smiling at him in a way that was meant to melt his knees. It worked.

The clubhouse was on a small rise and this time, as Jace helped her from the car, she took his arm. They walked in together and she smiled with delight as they were led to a table for two by the window. The setting was intimate and the view spectacular, but his eyes remained on her.

Mara thoroughly enjoyed the date. She held his attention completely, the food was superb, the view almost endless, and the ride home magical as they chatted easily about their notes, plans, and hopes for a smooth meeting the next day. As Jace walked her to the door, Mara lost her iron grip on her resolve and stepped into his arms.

He held her gently as he kissed her, fighting to keep from crushing her to him. Her lips were so soft and warm and they were sending chills and thrills through his body. He trembled with the effort to be gentle.

She smiled up at him as their lips parted.

"Get a room," growled a man carrying a six pack of beer, as he walked by to enter the apartment building.

"Piss off," replied Jace, still holding Mara in his arms.

"Jace, kiss me again," she said dreamily. "Kiss me like you mean it." She gave a slight gasp then a soft moan of delight as his hand touched the small of her back and pulled her tight to him. His mouth crushed her lips, hungry for her, all of her. She pressed herself tighter to him and opened her mouth to his exploring tongue. Mara felt his erection rise and push against her belly and she pressed herself tightly against it.

This time when their lips parted, he was on fire with lust, and it sent flutters of desire all through her body. It set her juices flowing and she stepped back from him, certain he could smell her desire. Mara swallowed hard as she fought to regain control. "Good night, Jace," she managed as she swallowed again.

"Mara..."

"Please let's not rush into anything..."

"You want to take it slow?"

"Please?"

"All right, but if you kiss me like that again, all bets are off." She could see how hard he was fighting to get back control himself.

Mara couldn't help herself; she stepped back into his arms once again. This time she got a real surprise. Rather than trying to kiss her again he just hugged her tightly. "Mara, if you want it slow, I'll do that," he breathed into her hair, "but just to be clear; I want you and I'm willing to do whatever it takes to win you. Please just tell me I have a chance here."

"I want you too, silly man," she replied softly, "but I want it to be more than lust. I want it to be real. I need for it to be real."

"Then we take it slow and let the love build," he replied, as he loosened his hold on her. "Tomorrow evening at the café?"

"Tomorrow evening," she replied, as she brushed her lips against his one last time before stepping away and disappearing into the building.

Mara stood before the mirror brushing her hair. A dreamy smile graced her lips and she hummed softly. "He said he wants me," she sighed to the woman in the mirror. "He wants me and is willing to take it slow to let the love build." Slowly she stopped and let the brush settle back to the counter top. Her smile faded as she gazed into the mirror.

"You've heard that before, Mara," said the woman in the mirror. "They're all willing to do it your way until they get what they want. Think, woman. Remember. Remember George? He swore undying love and showed that for several weeks once you moved in with him. Suddenly he was developing hobbies that didn't include you, his eyes began to wander, then his hands, and then..."

"Stop it," she said, as she slammed the hairbrush on the counter. "This is different. I know it is."

"Is it really? We'll see."

"Ohhhh..." Mara spun and angrily marched out to the living room where she found Meghan sitting on the sofa.

"Talking to yourself again?"

"Fighting with myself is more like it," sighed Mara, as she sank into a chair.

"Are you winning?"

"No."

"Okay, that's a bad sign," laughed Meghan. "Tell me about it. Did your date go sour?"

"No, it went perfect. It was all too perfect. When he kissed me I nearly tore off his clothes and jumped his bones right there. Damn, but he started my engines like nobody else ever has."

"So why wasn't the door locked and why isn't he in your bed all frazzled and snoring?"

Mara sighed again and looked away for a moment. "I've been broken hearted too many times, Meg. I promised myself it'd never happen again; that I'd wait until the real thing came along. I pulled back. I told him I wanted to take it slow, to be sure, to know it's love and not just lust."

Meghan sat up straight, all attention now, the mischief gone. "How did he take it, Sis?"

"He said he wants me, and he'll do whatever he must to prove that to me. He's willing to go slow as long as he's sure I'm not just playing with him."

"Wow." Meghan relaxed back into the cushions. "So, what was the self-fight all about?"

"Doubt. The voice of doom is trying to convince me that as soon as he has me in bed a few times he'll turn into another George and slowly wander off. Gods, Meg, I don't think I could take that again."

"Aw, honey, I know what you mean. Do you want me and the girls to give him the acid test?"

"You already did that the other night at the café. Meg, you're so damn sexy it's sickening, but he never paid you any attention. I was watching and his eyes were always on me. I have to confess I liked that, a lot."

"Oh, girl, you've got it bad," chuckled Meghan. "This guy's really gotten under your skin, hasn't he?"

Again Mara sighed and turned to gaze out the window. "Yeah, he has," she finally admitted.

"So what does your voice think of him?"

"What???"

"Mara, either we're both nuts or that voice is a real person, or something."

"It spoke to you?"

"It did. Sure creeped me out at first too, but I know it wasn't my imagination."

Mara leaned forward, eagerly searching her sister's face, her eyes. It was clear Meghan wasn't teasing. "How can you be sure?" she asked softly.

"Because I wouldn't do that shit to myself."

"Tell me."

"I was watching you and Jace and could see the sparks fly between you. I wondered if there was a man out there who would look at me with eyes like that. You know, not just looking for a roll in the hay, but just wanting to be in my space, wanting me in his. 'I wonder if there's a guy out there like that for me,' I asked. That's when I heard the voice, sort of soft and far away like. A woman's voice."

"Yes," breathed Mara. "What did it say?"

Meghan blushed softly and lowered her eyes. "It said he's coming, soon. It said to be aware of him and not lose my chance because this would be the one."

"Oh my god..."

"Yeah, I tried to ask a thousand questions, but I couldn't get it to speak again. I thought long and hard about coming over and stealing some of your meds."

"Why didn't you?" Mara sat back, relaxed again, a smile on her lips.

"Because, what if it's real? What if it's right and this is my one big chance to meet the right guy and be happy? To bring that special happiness to him, you know what I mean? Dammit, Mara, I want to be in love as badly as you do. Is that so wrong?"

"No honey, it's not wrong; it's natural. Everybody wants to be loved, to be in love and to share their life with a special someone."

"So what do we do?"

"Well, since we both hear it, as you say, we're both nuts or it's a real entity. I would prefer to think of it as a real entity. I say keep your eyes open and your smile polished. If I'm reading this right, your guy will show up tomorrow night."

"What? How the hell did you make that leap?"

"Four of Jace's cousins will be in town for the next couple of days. It just all seems to tie in too nicely, you know what I mean?"

"What do you know about these guys?" Meghan asked eagerly. "Are these the boys Jace was talking about?"

"Yes. They have a joint venture going on and plan to meet once a month in Higgston. If I read this right you'll meet your guy and still have lots of time to sort out all the feelings as you go along."

"Oh my god," breathed Meghan. "What else can you tell me?"

"Not much. These guys are all thirty-ish, single, and seem to do all right for themselves but they don't have jobs. Sorry sweetie, but it's not my place to tell you more."

"And there is more, isn't there, a lot more. Don't worry sis, if one of these guys is destined to fall for me I'll have the whole story out of him in a jiffy. Just tell me there's nothing illegal going on."

"No, no," laughed Mara. "Everything is on the up and up, but it's all personal business and for them to share or not."

"Has Jace shared with you?"

"Yes, he has, but I can't tell you anything more."

"Oh, this is so exciting," said Meghan, as she leaped to her feet. "Got any wine?"

"Nope, sorry."

"Tea then?"

"Sure, you put the kettle on," replied Mara, as she followed her sister to the kitchen. "So what's so damned exciting?"

"Mara, think about it," laughed Meghan, as she plugged in the kettle and took down the basket of teas. "We're not crazy, there are super sexy men all over the place, there's a mystery, and a ghost, witch, goddess, or whatever trying to guide us to happiness. Don't you think that's exciting?"

"Yes, and frightening too," smiled Mara, as she hugged her sister. "Meg, thanks for this. You always manage to find the silver lining."

"Silver lining? Girl, he took you out, paid attention to you, said he wants you and will do whatever it takes to win you, and then gave you a kiss that knocked your socks off. Where's the bad?"

"You're right," laughed Mara, as she hugged Meghan tighter then released her. "There is no bad, it's all good. Now make sure I remember that."

"I will. I promise."

JACE HARPER DROVE HOME on cloud nine. That kiss had rocked his world to the core. Jace had had a few liaisons in the past, but hadn't allowed himself to get too deeply involved, he'd been far too focused. However, he'd never been kissed like that before either.

Mara O'Grady's kiss had lit him on fire then turned up the heat. He had trembled all over and his knees had nearly failed him. The woman would never know how badly he'd wanted to put her back in the car, bring her back to the cottage, and tear off all her clothes.

"Gods," he muttered, as he parked the car. He was still trembling and weak from the power of the experience, "I'm doomed. I'm madly in love with the woman and terrified I'll bugger it up." He went in and kicked off his shoes and hung his jacket on a peg by the door. Jace drifted to the fridge, took out a bottle of water, and cracked it open.

"Dammit, I really don't want to mess this up, but I have no idea what to do."

"Call Morgan," whispered a soft voice in his mind.

Jace sobered up fast at that. Wary as a cat now, he tried and failed to get in touch with the voice again. Finally he gave it up "All right, lady ghost, I'll try it your way." As he spoke the words aloud a feeling of foreboding descended on him.

"So you don't like that idea, eh Gramps," he muttered, as he retrieved his phone from his jacket pocket, "then it must be the right thing to do after all." He dialled and waited.

"Morgan," said a deep voice, as the phone was answered on the fifth ring.

"Hey Morgan, it's Jace. How's it going?"

"Ah shit," sighed Morgan. He sounded like he had just woken up. "You've got woman troubles."

"How the hell could you know that?"

"Easy," chuckled that deep basso. "I'll be in town tomorrow, so most things could wait. You didn't yell, 'Morgan, I found it,' so no treasure. Therefore, you've got woman troubles."

"That's a fine piece of logic, Spock," sighed Jace, as he settled into the sofa, "and right on the money."

"Tell me all, my son. Confession is good for the soul."

"Forgive me, Morgan, for I have met an amazing woman and I have lustful thoughts."

"More than that, I'm thinking. You wouldn't call me on a matter of lust. Lefty can take care of that for you. This girl's gotten under your skin big time, right?"

"Right as rain," sighed Jace.

"Let me guess, she wants to go slow."

"Right again. So how do I do that without going crazy?"

"Spend time with her, Jace. Take her places, do things together. Pay attention to what she likes and what she doesn't. Get to know the girl inside the body, see if you really like hanging out with her.

"Show her she's important to you by listening to her; memorize the way she mixes her coffee, stuff like that. Don't get all over possessive or protective but be ready to stand up for her when she needs it.

"Second, get something else to love to take the edge off a bit."

"You mean like a teddy bear?"

"No, you moron, I mean a dog. The shelters are full of them and every damned one of them needs love. That's what dogs are. They're pack animals. A dog will love you unconditionally no matter what you do. Get one and learn how to do that by watching and learning."

"Morgan, how come you know so much about women?"

"I've got four older sisters, and we always had couple of dogs," chuckled that deep voice.

"Thanks, Morgan."

"Sure, anytime. See you tomorrow. Get some sleep."

"WHY, MEGHAN O'GRADY, don't you look fine today." That cheerful voice belonged to her friend and boss, Arlene. Meghan had just arrived to have coffee with the girls.

"Thank you, Arlene."

"What's the occasion?"

"I've given up waiting around. I have decided that today I'll meet the love of my life and I wanted to look good."

"Well you sure accomplished that," said Brittany, a good friend and the local hairdresser. "The rest of us are doomed; there won't be a man around who can see past you."

"Oh Brit, you say the sweetest things. Maybe you're the one. Snuggle over, kitten."

"Behave yourself," admonished Brittany, as she slid over to make room for Meghan. "Now, tell us what brought this on. What do you know that all us single girls need to know? Mara, do you know what she's up to?"

"Some of Jace Harper's cousins are due in town today," grinned Mara.

"Well, if they look anything like Jace, I can understand why Meg's all dolled up," said Arlene. "However, I'm deeply disappointed that the O'Grady girls didn't share that information with us in time for the rest of us to get ready."

"What, and give the competition an even chance?" asked Meghan. "Forget that, Arlene."

Suddenly there was the scream of a motorcycle engine gearing down. It turned into the parking lot and stopped. They all fell silent and watched the door as the sound of boots approached up the wooden steps. A tall man dressed in cobalt blue leather from head to toe came through the door. He was young and handsome with close-cut blonde hair and a dazzling smile. He nodded to the women, then chose a table at the other end of the room.

Arlene jumped to her feet and hurried over to serve him. "Hi there," he smiled, as she approached. "Coffee, lots of cream and sugar. What's my chances for a veggie omelette?"

"Better than average," she smiled. "That's coffee and a veggie omelette. Be right back."

"There he is, Meg," giggled Brittany. "Go get him."

"Nope, he's not the one," smiled Meghan.

"How do you know?"

"I'm an Irish witch and I know things," she grinned in reply. "I'll know the right one when he shows up."

As Arlene served the stranger, an old pick-up truck with an engine that had a deep sexy growl to it rolled in and parked. Again there was the thump of boots on the boards and all eyes turned towards the door.

The man who stepped through the door was a much different sight. He was about five foot ten with sandy brown hair that hadn't met a barber in some time. A three day scruff of beard graced his face; he looked dangerous. Then he smiled. Laugh crinkles around his eyes belied the aura of danger and there was only an air of mischief left.

Dressed in boots, jeans, and a T-shirt, he looked like most other men in the area. The difference was all the lean hard muscle. This man was accustomed to hard work. It showed in the callouses on his hands and the ease of his movements.

"This one, Meg?"

"No Brit, definitely not my type. I like tidy men."

"I think that might be a good thing; Arlene can't take her eyes off him."

"Oh yeah, he's Arlene's type," smiled Meghan.

The man looked around, spotted the motorcycle rider, and walked over to his table. "Morning, cousin, that your crotch rocket in the parking lot?" rumbled a voice so deep it almost came up from the floor.

"Hey, Morgan," grinned the man in leather, "how's it going?"

"Fair to middling, but I'm hungry as a bear and twice as mean."

"What'll it be?" asked Arlene, as she stood just out of his reach.

Morgan turned and got his first look at Arlene. His smile of delight said he liked what he saw. "Hi, I'll have some black coffee and that hungry man special I see on the board."

"Great. I'll be right back," sang Arlene, as she sped away.

"Oh my, that voice," sighed Britany. "That's even sexier than the sound of that truck engine."

"Behave yourself, Brittany," scolded Mara. "He'll hear you."

Just then there were more boots on the boards and three locals came in. They sat at a booth and the big one shouted for Arlene. "Arlene, get your pretty little ass out here and bring us some grub."

"I'll just be a minute," she replied in a cold voice, pouring up Morgan's coffee. As she went by the booth the man reached out and ran his hand under her skirt. She yelped and jumped away, spilling the hot coffee on her hands.

Morgan reached her in a heartbeat, taking the mug from her. "Quick now, run some cold water over that burn."

"I'm sorry I spilled..."

"Go on now, cold water. I'll get my own coffee."

He gently steered her towards the kitchen then turned to the men in the booth. They were staring at him when he threw the rest of the scalding coffee into the big man's lap. "Jesus Christ, asshole, that's hot!" The man exclaimed, as he leaped to his feet. Morgan's fist sank deeply into his solar plexus. The air whooshed from his lungs, and, making gasping sounds, the man sank slowly back into his seat. Morgan shoved him over and pushed in beside him.

"Now that really hurts, don't it?" grinned Morgan, as he shoved the man further over in the booth. "So fella, here's how it goes. I threw the coffee on your balls because you burned my girlfriend. I hit you for calling me an asshole. Are we done here, or does anybody else have something to say?" No one made a sound except for the labored breathing of his victim.

"No? Good, 'cause I'm starting to get cranky. So here's how it works. You all be quiet and make nice, nice. Dipshit here apologizes to Arlene; you eat your breakfast then haul your sorry asses out of here. Oh, and you'd better leave her a big tip for burning her."

The tall man in blue was standing beside the other bench of the booth. "Go sit down, Aiden," said Morgan. "Your food's getting cold. I got this." The man nodded and returned to his table. Morgan rose and went behind the counter, poured up another mug of coffee for himself then joined him.

"You always this cranky in the mornings?" asked Aiden, as Morgan sat down.

"Oh hell, I'm in a good mood today," chuckled Morgan.

Arlene appeared with his breakfast. "Thanks for that," she breathed softly.

"My pleasure, Arlene."

"How do you know my name?"

"It's on your name tag," he smiled. "Let me see that hand now." She placed her tiny hand in his calloused paw. It sent a tingle all through her as he gently inspected the damage. "Doesn't look like it went deep. Keep the cold water to it every chance you get today, and it should be fine. I'm Morgan Ross."

His eyes were twinkling with mischief, and he was still holding her hand. She blushed and left her hand where it was. "Did you say, girlfriend, Morgan?"

"Sorry," he grinned. "I thought it might make the boys more respectful."

"Do you have a girlfriend? Wife?"

"No, sadly I don't."

"Want one?"

"Was that an offer?"

"I come with kids."

"A bonus offer," he grinned, "I like that. We could give it a try if you like."

"I like," she replied. She was blushing furiously, but held his eyes.

"Then it's a deal," he rumbled. "Pass me your pad and pencil now."

"My pad and pencil?"

"As the boyfriend, I should lend a hand around here. Don't worry girl, I've waited tables before. You go join your friends over there while I take care of the customers."

She passed him the pad and pencil, then squeezed his hand. "Thank you."

Morgan just winked at her and returned to the booth with the three men. "Hi, I'm Morgan and I'll be your server for today. What'll it be boys?"

"The specials and coffee," one replied softly, not making eye contact.

"Coming right up," grinned Morgan, as he turned away to put in the order.

"Oh my god, Arlene, what did you just do?" asked Brittany, as Arlene re-joined her friends. "You don't even know this guy and you can see how dangerous he is."

"He's got gentle eyes," replied Arlene, "and that voice sends thrills right through me. I've been having a lot of trouble with those guys lately. I can't tell you why, but I instinctively trust Morgan. I know he likes me; I can feel it."

"But to ask him to be your boyfriend just like that..."

"I couldn't help myself," she replied, studying her hand. "He's just so damn strong, protective, and gentle; and suddenly I wanted that in my life. Is that so wrong?"

"No, it isn't, sweetie," smiled Mara, as she hugged her friend's shoulders. "It's all quite natural. I hope it works out for you." They watched as Morgan served the three men in the booth. It was clear he had waited tables before.

The girls had to get back to work, so Arlene went to sit with Morgan and Aiden. After the troublemakers had left, Morgan finished his breakfast, gave Arlene a huge tip, then asked directions to Jace's place. He and Aiden left together, the motorcycle spraying loose gravel as it sped from the parking lot. Late in the afternoon, two more men drifted in, had a snack, asked directions to the Harper place then left.

Meghan had given up by early afternoon and gone home, but the voice came again near dinner, so she freshened up and returned. The café was busy so she put on her apron to lend a hand. That's when they came in. Jace led the four cousins in and back to a table at the end of the room. It was the last available. Mara was with them.

Arlene started towards them, but Meghan stopped her. "Mine, all mine," she grinned as she headed for the group.

"Good evening, folks," she sang cheerily.

"You're working tonight?" asked Mara.

"Just this table," replied Meghan. She was standing to give the overly muscled Ira a good view of her charms.

"I'd say, by the drool on Ira's chin you're working more than that," chuckled Morgan. She made a face at him then laughed.

"Meghan, are you going to plague me again tonight?" asked Jace.

"Not if you live up to your promise." There was laughter in her voice and a twinkle in her eye and Ira was definitely smitten.

"All right," chuckled Jace. "Gentlemen, this is Mara's sister, Meghan O'Grady. "Meg, these are my cousins, Morgan Ross." Morgan nodded and winked as he spoke her name. "This one is Aiden Reilly, here is Logan Kerry, and this poor lad you have completely bedazzled is Ira Dunbar."

"It's a real pleasure to meet you, Ira." Meghan was giving him her best smile and it was having the desired effect.

He swallowed hard, then stood and took her offered hand in his huge one. "Make no mistake, the pleasure is mine," he replied with a boyish grin. "Tell me you're single."

"I'm single."

"Boyfriend?"

"Not until a minute ago."

"So you'll go out with me then?"

"I will."

"Meet you here tomorrow at ten?"

"I'll be here. Now, put me down so I can bring these starving folks a meal." There was lots of laughter and fun through the meal. Morgan introduced Arlene as his girlfriend to the rest of the group and she glowed in the attention.

After the meal, they left a generous tip then drove back to the mansion on the hill. Mara led them to the library where they gathered around the long table on the ground floor. Jace leaned his elbows on the table and spoke. "All right, guys. Let's get started. Has anyone found what we're looking for yet?"

No one had. Next they discussed some of the search methods, exchanging ideas, taking notes, etc. Finally, when there was little to add, Jace asked another question. "Has any of you had a burglar?"

They all looked at each other, shaking their heads. "What's up, Jace?"

"We've had a guy here," he replied, as he leaned back in his chair. "Twice. The first time Mara and I were standing over there and this big guy blasted out from behind the bookcase and nearly ran me down. I went after him, but he was way too fast on his feet.

"The second time was after Mara and I had dinner together. I came home and found him here again."

"Did you get him?" asked Ira.

"Nope, same thing again. The bastard sure is fast. I started a running program the next day. The thing is, I don't think he's found anything either."

"I don't think he's looking for the same thing we are," remarked Mara.

"What makes you think that?" asked Jace.

"Well, if none of the guys has seen him, that means he's focused on us. If he was looking for the same thing he should have made a try for one of the others."

"Then what the hell is he really after?"

"I'll bet he's after old Mr. Miller's gold."

"Miller's gold?" asked Morgan.

"This place was built by the Miller family," replied Mara, "and it was their home for several generations. That last Miller's grandfather was a real Scrooge according to all accounts. Apparently he hoarded gold coins, bars, jewelry, and whatever else he could get his hands on. After he died the grandson took up the hobby. After his death the hoard was never found and his heirs lived in poverty, so they say, eventually letting the place go for back taxes.

"The place stood empty for a few years then another man bought it. He only lived in it for a couple of months before he moved out. He never did anything to fix it up. Most folks figured he found the treasure then took off."

"That would have been Gramps," said Jace, as he gave her fingers a gentle squeeze. "He might have found it, but I think he had other things on the go here. He actually was a Miller and I doubt he ever lived in poverty."

"Either way, the guy's a pain in the ass you don't need," growled Morgan. "First thing tomorrow we should head out to the animal shelter and pick up a couple of dogs."

"Watch dogs at a shelter?"

"No, dummy, pets, friends, companions; they'll survive because you took them out of a kill shelter, and they'll be family. If Numbnuts comes back they'll drive him off."

"That makes sense to me," mused Jace. "Mara?"

"I love dogs, but I'm not allowed to have one in the apartment."

"All right, dogs it is. If there anything further?"

"Yes, there is," muttered Aiden, "and you all know it."

"Just what might that be?" asked Ira.

"The ghosts," replied Aiden. "Don't try to deny it, you've all felt them near and maybe the talker has even spoken to you."

"So, you hearing voices now, Aiden?" grinned Morgan.

"So have you, Morgan," he replied, "deny it if you can."

"I can't," sighed Morgan. "Anybody else?"

Slowly everyone else raised their hand. "Yeah, I thought so," said Aiden. "I have two. One is just nasty and gives me the shivers every time I start to search for the prize. The second one whispers to me every once in a while. She wants me to find it. What do you guys hear?"

"Much the same thing," replied Jace. "We've taken to calling old creepy, Gramps. I have no idea who or what the woman is, but she seems helpful."

"That sounds about right," said Logan. "I get the feeling those two have been at logger heads for a long time."

"Yeah," said Ira, "and I get the feeling there's more going on for them than just our quest."

"I get the impression our quest will settle whatever it is between them," Jace mused. "Just an impression, but there it is."

"Makes sense," said Morgan, "otherwise why help us at all? I'd say solving this thing should put old creepy Gramps to rest forever and let her rest. That, or she just wants to piss him off."

"Either way around," grinned Jace, "I'm all for it." There was a round of laughing agreement at that. They chatted for a while longer, but then the meeting broke up.

Jace walked Mara home under the stars. She had linked their arms but seemed to be lost in thought. "Penny," smiled Jace.

"What? Oh, yes, sorry. I was lost in thought; thinking about our ghosts. I think there is more going on here than the quest. I want to spend some more time in the town Library and archives researching that old house. I'd really like to know what the heck is going on."

"That makes sense to do," he replied. "If we've got ghosts with issues then the root of those issues must lie in the past somewhere. It would be nice to have some answers; maybe you'll find something to help us with the search."

"I'll start first thing tomorrow."

"Good idea, because right now you've got something else to do."

"I do?"

"You do," he breathed softly, as he stopped and pulled her close.

Mara thrilled to the pressure of his hand on the small of her back, pinning her tight against him. His lips sought hers and her arms encircled his neck as she lifted up for the kiss. Thrills ran through her as he crushed his mouth to hers hungrily. She felt the heat rise in her core and her juices begin to flow. His arousal swelled hard against his jeans and pressed against her belly, sending more thrills through her.

When the kiss ended she grabbed his jacket tightly in her fists and pushed back to arm's length. Both were breathing heavily, their bodies alive with desire. "Dammit, Jace Harper," she panted. "I said I wanted to... oh hell." She pulled hard on his jacket, forcing her body tightly against his once again, locking her lips on his and probing with her tongue.

His hands locked on her firm butt as he responded to the kiss, pulling her closer and rubbing his hard-on against her belly. Her hand dropped down to grip him through the jeans and he groaned as he broke the kiss and pushed her gently back.

"Stop it, Mara," he gasped. "If you want love before lust you'd better stop right now before I lose all self-control."

Mara fought for control of her breathing, and then gazed into his eyes. "Dammit, Jace Harper, what are you doing to me?"

"Not a damn thing," he replied. "Curse the luck. Come here; let me hold you."

She came willingly into his arms and rested her head on his chest. "Jace, thank you for that."

"I hate myself."

"Why?"

"Because cold showers suck, that's why. Come on, let me take you home."

She giggled and the mood was broken.

They reached her door and he pulled her close once more, but the kiss was gentle, sweet, and she savored the tenderness of it. "Goodnight, my darling," she whispered, before she stepped out of his arms and disappeared inside the building. Still a bit shaken by the power of the emotions that had gripped him, Jace turned his steps homeward.

Upping the Game

Jace Harper stripped off and climbed into bed. With the taste of Mara's kiss still on his lips, he relieved the sexual tension in his body then drifted off to sleep. He awakened in the night, screaming. "A dream," he muttered aloud, "just a fucking dream. Gramps, you rotten bastard, I'll exorcise you for this, I swear it." He rose and padded to the kitchen.

Grabbing the peanut butter jar he spread a healthy portion on a piece of bread then poured a tall glass of milk. His hands were trembling as he lifted the glass to his lips. Jace swore and paced about as he finished the food, but it calmed him enough to think straight. "Write it down, have to write it down."

He returned to the bedside table and retrieved the book he'd bought for a dream journal. With pen in hand he sat to the kitchen table and began to write. He marked the date then began to describe the dream.

"Another nightmare. Dark, damp place. The same man that shot the poor guy last time. This time he had Mara chained to a wall, naked. He wanted something from me, but when I couldn't understand he lashed her bare body with a horse whip. Mara's screams ripped the heart from me, but I was helpless to stop him. I woke up to screams; my own, not hers."

Jace thought for a minute, then set the pen down and folded the book. "We must have hit on something at the meeting last night," he mused. "I think we've got Gramps on the run. I need to review everything we said last night. The clue is in there somewhere." With that in mind he returned to bed. This time he did dream of Mara, but this was a completely different dream. It was the one he'd wanted in the first place.

While Jace slept and fought his battles, Mara lay awake, tossing and turning. She tried to relieve herself, but the orgasm didn't do it. Her ache for Jace Harper went much deeper. "Dammit, Mara," she railed at herself, "you're the one who demanded to go slow, to be sure, and yet, tonight, you had him in your hand quick enough. If you keep sending mixed signals like that he'll either run away or rape you.

"You know he wants you; you do. He's the one who backed off tonight, but he sure didn't want to. He's the stronger one here. Jace wants you, Mara, and he's trying to play it your way to get you. Cut the man some slack or jump his bones before he goes completely crazy; or before we do."

Vowing to do just that the next time they got hot and heavy, Mara finally drifted off to sleep.

The next morning Mara spent most of her time in the archives, searching, but she had no real idea what she was searching for. She was late getting to lunch at the café. There was no sign of Jace, but Morgan was there waiting tables.

"Funny," she thought, "he's not half so scary when you get to know him a bit. I wonder what his story is. Ah well, that's for another time."

She sat with Meghan and Ira, chatted easily through lunch, and then returned to the archives. Mara's fresh notebook was filling up fast as she worked.

She didn't see or hear from Jace that day and was a bit hurt by that, more than she wanted to admit. The next morning, after a quick breakfast, Mara hurried off to the library. She had more research to do. She arrived at the library to find a rose and a note hanging on the doorknob. Opening the note, she read it with a slightly bemused smile.

"Mara, sorry I got lost in space yesterday. Love Jace."

"I'll confess I was a bit hurt, Jace Harper," she mused, as she inhaled deeply of the rose's delightful perfume. "However, I'll forgive you since you suck up so sweetly." She was smiling brightly as she stepped inside and turned the sign on the door from CLOSED to OPEN. She spent most of the morning serving customers and going over her notes. As soon as Louise arrived Mara abandoned her for the archives once again.

Jace called just before closing time and Mara sat back rubbing the kinks from her neck as she answered the phone. "Library."

"Hi, Mara, it's Jace, are you mad at me for deserting you?"

"No, you suck up real sweet. I think I'll keep you."

"Great," he chuckled. "Can I cook you dinner tonight at the cottage? I have some new friends I want you to meet."

"Okay, give me a half hour to get home and freshen up."

"Perfect. I'll have the barbeque going out back. Don't bother knocking, just come on through."

Mara closed up and hurried home to shower and change. At first she pulled on her tightest jeans, push up bra, and a top that showed off a lot more cleavage than she would normally show. She started for the door then thought better of it.

"Meeting new people, Mara," she muttered as she changed into a regular bra and a looser fitting T-shirt. "I'm keeping the jeans on, dammit." Satisfied, she headed for the door once again and again, she turned back. "Make up Mara, just enough to be presentable."

Finally satisfied with her appearance, she raced out the door and hopped aboard her aging car. A short drive later, she parked at the cottage and went around the house. A dog suddenly leaped to its feet and barked. She stood facing an old pit bull terrier. She gulped as a second one appeared from behind a lawn chair.

"Hey, Scoot, Billy, relax," sang Jace, as he emerged from inside carrying steaks and potatoes wrapped in foil, "this is Mara; she's part of our pack. Just let them sniff you, Mara, but don't try to touch or talk to them until they tell you it's okay."

"I know," she smiled, as she remained in place. "I grew up with dogs."

Mara stood still and the dogs sniffed all around her. When the inspection was done she felt a warm muzzle in her hand. A moment later she was on her knees, hugging the two warm bodies with wagging tails. "You're good boys, yes you are," she cooed, as she rubbed the bellies suddenly presented for just that action.

"So, where did you get these tough guys from?" she asked, still rubbing.

"From the shelter," he replied, as he applied the steaks to the barbeque. "Billy, the bigger one, was being led to the gas chamber when Morgan and I got there. Scoot had been abused and then abandoned. He was due to be put down today."

"They're not pups, Jace," she said, as she rose to her feet and joined him at the barbeque.

"I know. Puppies often get adopted, but old dogs just get ignored and put down. I can imagine what it's like to be tossed aside like so much garbage. It's not their fault they got old."

"I know," she replied, as she reached down to pet Scoot once again. "You give it your best shot, Scoot, and they just push you aside when you become inconvenient. It sucks."

"Whoa, that had an edge to it," Jace said softly.

"Life lessons learned the hard way. So, you have a soft spot for old dogs, do you?"

"Not really. It was the way Morgan explained it, much like you just did. He said these guys have a lifetime of experience and they'll know full well how good they have it. It sounded reasonable so I brought them home. I spent the day with them, bonding. It didn't take long to see the wisdom of it all."

"Tell me," she smiled. Mara noticed the way both dogs went to Jace and checked in before lying back down in the sun. She also liked the way he touched each one to reassure him that all was well.

"You said we need security at the big house. We spent a lot of time in there yesterday, and wandering around the property. That way they'll accept it as part of their territory too."

"Are they going to sleep there at night?"

"Oh, hell no. They're staying with me."

"Now that had an edge to it as well, sir. Tell me."

"It's nothing , Mara, really."

"Liar, liar, pants on fire."

"All right." He sighed as he closed the barbeque lid and put his arms around her. "I'll confess that was my original thought, but last night changed my mind."

"Why? What happened?"

"The other night, when we got a bit carried away..." Jace sighed and pulled her closer, resting his chin on her head. "When we got hot and heavy and I almost came unglued, I had another nightmare. This time the murderer had you chained to a wall, naked. When I couldn't understand what he wanted, he whipped you. Your screams tore out my heart, Mara. I couldn't stop him."

"Oh, Jace," she whispered, as she kissed his cheek and held him. "It was just a nightmare."

"No, honey, it was more than that," he replied, taking a deep shuddering breath. "It was an attack. Anyway, last night it came again, but this time, in the dreams, two wolves came and chased him away. In the dream I got you free and the wolves curled up beside us. When I woke up these guys were beside the bed with their chins resting on my arm. I believe that somehow, they managed to interfere with what was attacking me."

"In that case, they stay with you." Mara kissed his cheek again, then knelt to hug the dogs again. "That's your job, guys. You have to protect

Jace when I'm not here to do it." She was swiftly losing her make-up to slobbery dog kisses.

They chatted easily through the meal. Jace laughed as Scoot flipped Mara's arm with his nose causing her to spill barbeque sauce on her shirt. Scoot tried to look contrite as she scolded him, but his wagging tail gave him away. "You're a complete beast," she admonished, as she scratched him under the chin. "Yes you are, you as bad as that Jace Harper. It's a good thing for both of you that you're cute. I could never stay mad at cute."

Afterwards, Mara helped Jace with the washing up, then went to the bathroom to see if she could get the stain out of her shirt. She failed, but she found something interesting, the book he was reading. She returned to the great room, book in hand.

"The Principles of Witchcraft and Basic protection spells?" she asked, holding up the book. "Jace?"

"I found it in our library," he sighed, as he sank into the sofa. "Where the hell else am I supposed to turn, Mara? If I tell anyone else about the nightmares I'll get locked up in a rubber room."

"I agree," she said, as she sat at the other end of the sofa, facing him. "This place could do with a good cleansing. I mean the cottage as well as the main house. I think we could use some help."

"Help?"

"My cousin and her husband are Wiccans. They have a small occult shop over in Springfield. I could call them, find out the cost."

"Cost?"

"They have to earn a living too, Jace."

"Yeah, you're right. Just because I don't understand how it works doesn't mean it has no value. I couldn't fix a car either because I don't understand how the engine works, but I'd expect to pay the mechanic. To hell with the cost, Mara. We need this done; call your cousin."

"I'll call her first thing tomorrow," smiled Mara. "Meanwhile, keep the boys here close. If Gramps wants to play rough then we'll get rough. You know, we must be getting close if he's coming on that strong."

"That was my thought. He got tough the night of the meeting. We must have hit on something there. Now we just have to figure out what it was."

"We will," she smiled. Jace's unconscious use of *we* instead of *I* was giving her a warm feeling. *"He's thinking of us as a couple. Thank god for that, because I was afraid it was just me."*

"I made some notes that night," she smiled. "I have the book in my bag; I thought you might want to review them." Mara rose gracefully and retrieved her bag from the chair where she's dropped it. Pulling out the notebook, she returned and sat close, pressing her body snugly against him. Jace smiled and put his arm around her shoulders. He lightly kissed her head as she opened the book.

They sat that way for some time, reviewing the notes, discussing the possibilities, and just enjoying the closeness, the tender warmth of it. The spell was finally broken when Billy whined to get out. Jace took the dogs outside and Mara made herbal tea. When he returned they sat at the table, sipping the tea and continuing their conversation. It was domestic and so very delicious to Mara.

Jace watched her as she cleaned up after the tea, a smile on his face. The girl set his pulse racing, and yet she was wonderful company. "Penny," she said, as she noticed the contented smile he was beaming her way.

"I was just thinking how much I've enjoyed this evening; how much I enjoy your company. I could cheerfully make a habit of this."

She smiled with delight, but her reply was lost in the wail of sirens. The fire truck sped by with a police car close behind. Mara's phone began to ring insistently. "Mara. What??? Oh no...I'm on my way."

"Mara, what is it? What's happened?"

"The library's on fire; I have to go."

"I'm coming too."

"No, Jace, you have to stay here to reassure the boys that it's okay. See, they're getting upset. There's nothing either of us can do now, but I have to be there. I'll call as soon as I know what the damage is."

Mara fled the house and leaped aboard her car. Loose gravel sprayed away from the wheels as she raced towards the heart of town. Jace pulled on his jacket and took the dogs out. They jogged up to the main house where he'd have a better view. He could see the smoke rising in the distance; the town library was definitely on fire. He sat on the steps of the front porch, the dogs beside him, watching helplessly.

Darkness fell slowly and the dogs lay down beside him and went to sleep. "Ah, the wisdom of old dogs," he smiled as he stroked their sleeping forms. "When you can't do anything else, might as well nap." Just then his phone buzzed.

"Harper."

"Jace, it's Mara. They've about got the fire out, but the smoke damage is horrible." She was crying. "I doubt I'll be able to salvage anything."

"Mara, come home now."

"What?"

"Come home to me and the boys, you don't need to be alone right now. Please? I promise I'll be on my best behavior."

"Okay," she sniffed. "I'm sorry to come apart like this, Jace. It's just that I built up that library from almost nothing and..."

"I know, honey, I know. Drive carefully now. Come home so I can hold you."

"You're a right bastard, Jace Harper," came a voice in his mind, *"she's vulnerable right now; you're taking advantage."*

"You shouldn't judge others by your own standards, Gramps," growled Jace, as he rose to his feet. Both dogs jumped up as well and followed as he strode around the house and down the hill.

He was waiting outside the door as she arrived. Mara leaped from the car and ran into his waiting arms, sobbing her heart out. Suddenly she pushed out of his arms and, turning to the house on the hill, raised her middle finger in salute. "It won't help you, you old bastard. You're too late. All you've done is free me up to spend every day here searching."

Mara was trembling with rage now, but melted again as Jace's arms enfolded her once again. "Mara?"

"Yeah?"

"What makes you think Gramps had something to do with this?"

"I could feel him there, Jace, gloating. He thought he stopped me, but he was wrong."

"What do you mean?"

"There's an old escape tunnel under the house, and a room somewhere within it. It was built by the original owner, Phidias Tomlinson to hide in and escape if the place was attacked or if the slaves revolted. It was built by slave labor and after it was built, there was a fire in the slave pens. None survived. He may have destroyed my archives, but I can rebuild most of them."

"You can?"

"Oh yes, town records, county records, places like that, land registry offices, they all keep records. That'll give me most of it; the rest is probably in our library anyway. I'll have to start from scratch, and it'll take years, but I will rebuild it. I swear I will."

"So, you're saying Gramps isn't my grandfather, but someone else?"

"Both, Jace. I'll trade the story for a cuddle and a glass of wine."

"That's a deal," he laughed, as he suddenly swept her up in his arms and carried her inside. He deposited her on the sofa then went to pour her a glass of the wine he'd bought to have with dinner but had forgotten about. He returned and passed her the glass, then sat beside her and cuddled her into his arms. "All right, pretty lady, story time. Talk to me."

Mara took a sip of the wine and set the glass on the coffee table. She relaxed back into his arms as she began the story. "A lot of it was in the archives, and some is local legend. I kept it in a separate notebook as I didn't think it completely relevant to our search. I wanted it for the history of Higgston I plan to write.

"It began with a man named Phidias Tomlinson. He arrived in this area in the late sixteen/early seventeen hundreds. He was rich, ambitious, and deeply religious. He soon gained a lot of influence in the local church and that gained him even more power. A poor farmer had two daughters and gave the eldest to Tomlinson in marriage to clear a debt.

"Now here's where we get away from the main line and into an old local legend, but I believe there is a core of truth in it. It's said the girls were witches. The youngest married a poor man who had the audacity to refuse Tomlinson's offer for his land. Tomlinson applied pressure to the church council and the young woman was accused of witchcraft.

She hid when Tomlinson and his men came for her. Her husband refused to give her up and Tomlinson killed him."

"Like in the dream," mused Jace.

"Yes, like the dream; that's what started me on this path. Anyway, the girl is said to have killed herself beside her husband's body, and cursed Tomlinson as she died. The elder sister found them and cursed her husband as well.

Tomlinson believed he had a quiet obedient wife, but he didn't. She continued to amplify the curse until the day he died. On his death bed she revealed herself to him and cursed him again. His twisted soul is bound to this world and to his line. From that time, each male descendant has been afflicted with his greed, malice, and avarice as well as the madness that drove him.

"Her spirit has lingered as well to make sure it sticks. The curse ends when there is no direct male descendant, but only female. The male children of that female generation will uncover his misdeeds and bring them to light. In doing so, they gain all the wealth accumulated over the generations and none of the madness. Instead they will inherit the gentle loving nature of the younger witch."

"Of the younger witch?"

"Yes, remember, the witches were sisters. Every madman in Phidias Tomlinson's line was also descended from the elder sister."

"So you think, Gramps is Tomlinson?"

"Both," replied Mara, as she snuggled deeper under his protective arm, "and the same."

"So, the second voice is the witch?"

"Yeah, I think so."

"But you said you've been hearing her for years. What would be that connection?"

"I've been thinking about that. The voice always encouraged me to read... more, to study, the history of Higgston. I think she was trying to prepare me for your coming, knowing you'd need help."

"Okay, but why talk to Meghan?"

"I think she's been talking to several women," replied Mara. "I'm willing to bet she's talked to Arlene too."

"So somewhere out there are two more women who think they're crazy, but their real purpose is to help us?"

"I think so, but I think our purpose is more, Jace. With the history of madness in your family, I think she's chosen strong women to help keep you balanced."

"Oh yeah? Keep me from going off the deep end, you mean?"

"Yes," she giggled, "I was chosen to keep you sane."

"Then why the hell are you driving me crazy?"

"It's part of the therapy." She giggled again and Jace took the empty wine glass from her hand and set it back on the coffee table beside the nearly empty bottle. She'd been sipping while she talked, and he'd kept the glass full for her.

"Yeah? Well part of your therapy is a good night's sleep. You go do your thing and I'll turn down the bed for you."

He stood her on her feet and shooed her towards the bathroom. She came out a few minutes later, all giddy and smiling seductively at him, batting her eyelashes furiously and dressed only in one of his T-Shirts. Jace scooped her up and carried her to the bedroom. "Turn it down, Mata Hari," he smiled as he tucked her in.

"Jace," she sighed, "come to bed with me."

"All right," he replied, as he pulled the covers up over her then lay down beside her.

"I meant under the covers with me, silly."

"I know, but not tonight, not this way, Mara my magical woman. If, after the hangover has worn off, you still have that in mind I'll be thrilled to accept. After all, it is my one of my favorite fantasies."

"Oh yeah? Tell me some of the others."

"No. Now go to sleep," he chuckled.

"I used your toothbrush," she giggled, as she snuggled closer and closed her eyes.

"Brat." He smoothed her hair with a gentle hand and kissed her forehead. "Go to sleep."

The downer experienced after the adrenalin dump from the excitement and the wine soon took effect and Mara was sound asleep. Jace kissed her again and rose from the bed. He stepped outside with the dogs while they did their last bit of business for the day, then called them in.

Mara awakened to a throbbing headache and the worst case of dry mouth she'd had in years. She groaned softly as she struggled upright and padded off to the bathroom. Jace was asleep on the sofa, both dogs on the floor beside him. They lifted their heads as she re-emerged in her jeans and stained shirt. She sighed and went to the door.

Tails wagging, they headed out for their morning business. Mara stood in the doorway shielding her eyes from the bright sunlight. She heard Jace moving around somewhere then the toilet flushed. A few moments later the boys returned, and she let them in. Jace already had their food bowls down and waiting. The coffee pot was also gurgling a welcome song.

"Good morning, pretty lady," he sang. She winced and held her finger to her lips then waggled it at him. "Oops, sorry," he whispered loudly and grinned.

Mara pointed at the empty wine bottle and sighed. "Did I do that all by myself?" she asked softly.

"Yup, you did."

"I am so disappointed in you, Jace Harper."

"Oh? Because I got you drunk?"

"Because you got me tipsy and didn't take advantage of me."

"Oh, sorry, my bad; I'll remember that next time."

"Next time just skip the booze and ravish me. I'd far rather wake up with you in the bed than alone with a hangover."

"Mara..."

"No, no. It's time to speak plainly...and softly," she groaned, as she carefully lowered herself into a chair at the table.

"Mara..."

"No, Jace, listen to me. I've had too many men in my life who wanted only one thing, then they tossed me aside like an old boot." Scoot nudged her elbow and she put her arm around him for a doggy hug. "Just like these guys, I gave my all and it wasn't returned."

"Okay, and that's relevant how?"

"Last night the tables were turned," she sighed. "It was me who needed someone, and you were there for me. You cared for me and didn't take advantage where you could have. I'd like a lot more of that in my life."

"Mara, are you sure you don't want to wait until you're feeling better to have this discussion?"

"No, I want to do this now. Jace Harper, you said you wanted me. Did you mean it?"

"With all my heart and hormones," he breathed.

"I feel the same," she replied as she reached for his hand. "I'm yours if you want me."

"I do want you, Mara, but I want you forever. I realized last night how badly I want this to be forever. We can go as fast or slow as you want as long as I get to keep you."

"So take me now."

"Oh no, girl. Now I'm making you breakfast. You need a day or two to get back up to speed first. Mara, don't get me wrong here, but..."

"You've had way too much experience with hangovers?"

"My dad was a drunk. I've seen a lot of hangovers. I want you; I want you to come to me when you're ready, and I don't want to see regrets on your face three days later."

"Is that why you didn't drink any last night?"

"I've been drunk only once in my life, never again."

"That sounds like a lesson learned the hard way."

"It was. I promised myself I'd get debt free before I ever drank then I'd try it once to see what the magic was for my father. I got really stupid, then falling down drunk. I puked my lungs out in a hotel bathroom and woke up in the bathtub. It took three days before I was normal again. I made a lot of idle promises during those three days, but I learned. Now I drink coffee or root beer."

"So you think I'll change my mind in a few days."

"Oh god, Mara, I hope not."

"But you have to know for sure." He just nodded.

"All right," she sighed, "we'll play it your way, but if I don't get laid by Saturday night, I'll shoot you. Now, since you won't jump my bones, how about that breakfast."

"Bacon, sausages, and runny eggs?" he grinned as he pushed away from the table and stood up.

"God will get you for that, Jace Harper, and so will I. There's a special hell for people who tease the infirm."

"I'd heard that," he grinned. "How about some toast with jam and coffee."

"Sounds perfect."

Slowing it Down

Breakfast did make Mara feel better. She went home to shower and put on clean clothes while Jace took the dogs for a run. The shower also helped to improve Mara's state of mind. She blew her hair dry, then sat on the end of the bed facing the mirror. It was going to be another one of those talk to yourself sessions and she knew it had to happen. It was the only way to get her thoughts straight.

Looking at the woman in the mirror, she sighed deeply. "What the hell are you looking at?"

"I'm looking at a pathetic wimpy puss, that's what. Tell me you didn't beg Jace Harper to jump your bones? Tell me he didn't turn you down. Tell me you didn't tell him he could have you anytime he wants. Tell me you're not nuts or just too needy to think straight."

"Okay, I admit I did all those things, but I'm not crazy."

"No?"

"Well, maybe I'm crazy over Jace Harper, but that's all. No one's ever done for me what he did last night. He could have had me, and I'd have welcomed it. Dear god, I get butterflies in my belly every time he gets near me. When he kisses me I don't even know what world I'm on.

"Dammit, I know I'm in lust, but I'm starting to think I'm really in love too. This time it's different."

"So how is it different? You promised yourself you'd be the one being pursued this time, not the one doing the chasing, yet here you are, throwing yourself at Jace Harper."

"Yeah, you've got me there. I tried to play it cool, but every time he gets close all I can think of is jumping his bones. What the hell am I supposed to do? He's so damned gorgeous, tall, strong..."

"There you go again."

"What am I supposed to do?" she asked again, as tears began to leak from her eyes.

Suddenly the voice returned to her mind unbidden. "Relax Mara, breathe deeply and relax."

"You're not supposed to talk to me," she sniffed.

"You seem like you need a friend."

"So, you're my friend?"

"I am, and always have been."

"All right friend, tell me what to do because everything I try has fallen flat."

"You underestimate yourself, Mara," chuckled the voice. "Think back over some conversations with Jace Harper. You were adamant about going slow until you were sure he truly loves you, that the connection is more than lust. He agreed to those terms. Even when you were ready to throw the rules out the window, he wasn't.

"Mara O'Grady, this man wants you, he's said as much several times. He's respected your boundaries, went out of his path to make sure you'd forgiven him for an imagined sleight, and he supported you when you needed him."

"So what do I do? Do I really deserve this guy?"

"Yes, you do, and he truly needs you. Mr. Harper is a long way from anything he truly understands. He needs your strength, Mara."

"So what do I do?"

"Stop trying so hard. Let him come to you."

"Go back to the original plan?"

"Yes, because he can function there, but stay alert for an opportunity to claim him completely."

"How do I do that?"

"The same way women have been doing it forever." The voice sounded like it was smiling as it withdrew from her consciousness.

Mara sat mulling it all over for a few moments then she spoke to the mirror again. "You have to help me and stop picking on me."

"All right," smiled the woman in the mirror, "let's see, it's a warm day, let's start with short shorts and a push up bra. Let's give the man a peek at the prize to whet his appetite." Alas it was not meant to be. Her phone began to ring.

"Mara O'Grady."

"Hi Mara, it's the chief of the volunteer fire department here. There's an insurance investigator in town and he wants to talk to you. Are you free this morning?"

"It's nearly lunch time; I'll meet him at the Cozy Café since my office is a mess right now."

"That would be perfect," he chuckled. "When can we expect you?"

"Give me twenty minutes, Chief. I'll be right along."

Instead of the sexy she'd wanted to show Jace, Mara arrived at the café in a long skirt, blouse buttoned to the top, glasses instead of contacts, and her hair up in a bun. She wasn't wearing make-up. Mara was in full librarian mode.

Mara called Jace as she was leaving the apartment for her meeting. "Watch those guys, Mara, they can be real snakes."

"Oh?"

"Yeah, I used to be one. Do you need me to be there with you?"

"No, that won't be necessary, Jace. You and the boys have fun without me, and I'll call again when it's over."

"All right, men," sighed Jace, "looks like we're on our own for a while. Give me an honest opinion, would you? Should I have taken her up on her offer last night? Yeah, I know you guys sure would have, but then, you're a couple of hounds." Both dogs wagged their tails and rubbed against his legs. They had no idea what he was talking about, but he was giving them affection, something both dogs craved deeply. They returned it in kind.

"The thing is, guys, she drives me crazy. One minute she wants to go slow and the next I think I'm about to get ravished. Yeah, I know, I should be so lucky." Jace flopped into his chair by the window and the dogs lay down at his feet.

"All right, men, it's time to put our thinking caps on again. Let's face some reality here. We'll never understand women; we just won't, so we have to accept that. Now, having said that, what should we do next, besides dream about and drool over Mara O'Grady? We need to occupy ourselves; let's focus on the quest for a minute.

"There's a secret room under the place somewhere. That part is intriguing. Should we go tear the place apart looking for that? No, it's always been there; it's not going anywhere. Besides, there's no guarantee that Gramps ever knew about it or found it. It might hold old Miller's treasure, but the real quest is for something else, Grandpa's treasure.

"All right, now we set a few priorities. Miller's treasure can wait a bit. That's our fallback position if the real quest becomes a bust. We have four other guys depending on us, the group quest comes first. We should focus our efforts there."

Jace rose to his feet and the dogs jumped up too, ready for whatever adventure he planned next. Together they marched up to the main house. Once in the library, the dogs were soon bored and looking for a place to nap.

Jace was another matter. He set to work on another bookcase. First, he emptied it and pulled it out. The inspection of the floor and wall below and behind the case proved fruitless, so he pushed it back into place and sat to the table. He began working his way through the books. It was hours later when his phone rang.

"Harper."

"It's Mara."

"Hi, how did it go?"

"It's still going."

"You're serious."

"I am. This gentleman is practically accusing me of setting the place on fire to collect the insurance money to build a bigger library."

"Asshat. Put me on speaker."

"Go ahead," said Mara.

"Mr. Harper."

"Yes."

"This young woman has told me quite a tale of your generosity. I'd just like to confirm a few of the details."

"First things first," replied Jace. "Have you provided Miss O'Grady with your full name, your position with the company, and the name of your supervisor as well as a contact number for said supervisor?"

"Well, no, I..."

"Do so now, I'll wait." A moment went by, then Mara spoke.

"Got it, Jace."

"Good, now hang up and call that supervisor. Confirm this man's identity. If he checks out call me back, if not, call the police." Jace clicked off the call. Ten minutes later his phone rang again.

"Jace, it's Mara. He checked out."

"Put me on speaker. Is there anyone else there with you to witness the conversation, Mara?"

"Right here, Jace," rumbled Morgan's deep voice.

"All right, ask your questions."

"Mr. Harper, Miss O'Grady as told me you own a rather extensive library, a private collection."

"I do."

"She says you've promised to give it to her, but she's given me no reason to believe this might be true. Why would you do that, sir?"

"Wedding present to my bride," replied Jace. "Is there anything further?"

"I, ah, well, I guess not at the moment, but I may want to interview Miss O'Grady again."

"Any further interviews will be conducted in the presence of an attorney," replied Jace. "Morgan, please escort Mara to her car."

"She walked, Jace," replied Morgan. "I'll put her in the truck and bring her to you."

"Thanks, Morgan. I'm in the library on the hill."

"On our way."

Mara gave Morgan a look of gratitude and pointed at the restroom sign. He nodded as she stepped away. Once she disappeared, he spoke. "Listen buddy," growled Morgan, as he leaned across the table, "you've put that girl through the wringer for over two hours and come up empty. All you've got is your boss telling you to find a way out of paying the policy. It's time to back off."

"Are you threatening me?"

"No, you moron, Jace Harper already did that. Harper's got more money than God. He'll land on your head with a battery of lawyers and grind your ass into mutton. He'll leave you begging on the street and not even know he's spent pocket change. Take my advice, stay away from Harper's woman."

Morgan straightened up and Mara was right at his side. She linked her arm through his. "I'm ready to go, Morgan."

Morgan winked at Arlene and took Mara out to his truck. A moment later it growled and pulled out of the parking lot. "I heard what you said to that man. Morgan Ross, you're a terrible liar," giggled Mara.

"No I'm not," he grinned in reply. "I'm damned good at it. Did you see his face? He's a beaten man. Now he'll try to find some other way to weasel out of paying the policy, but he'll leave you alone. Besides, it wasn't all lies."

"No?"

"Not at all. You are Jace's woman; deny it if you can."

"I am, or I would be if he'd just... I just don't know for sure what he's thinking."

"He'll probably tell me the same about you," he grinned. "Cut the poor boy some slack, Mara. You're all he thinks about. The sooner you two get it together the sooner he can get back to business."

"Oh, just like you?"

"Ow, that went straight for the heart. Yeah, just like me. Guess I should stop hanging around Higgston and get my ass back to business, shouldn't I?"

"No, Morgan. I know you have to go back soon, but stay a few more days, please. I've never seen Arlene so happy and yet flustered at the same time. It looks good all over her."

"Yeah? Well, maybe I can spare a few more days at that," he chuckled. "Here we are, Harper's Hill, safe and sound."

"Are you coming in?"

"I'd just be in the way."

"Can't wait to get back to Arlene?"

"Busted. See you later, Mara."

"Thanks again, Morgan," smiled Mara, as she closed the truck door and watched him drive away. As he reached the bottom of the hill she turned and entered the house. "Jace?"

"In the library, sweetheart."

She found him on the second floor, seated at the table full of neat rows of books. There were notes on the rows, top shelf, second shelf, and so on. "Oh my, how very organized of you, Mr. Harper. I am impressed."

"Good," he grinned, as he leaned back in the chair and rubbed at his neck. "I'm trying to impress you."

"It's working. May I ask what brought this on?"

"I just picked up where we left off, Mara. We still have the bottom floor to do and it's a lot bigger."

"Yes it is. I guess I just expected you to be exploring in the basement, looking for that hidden tunnel and room."

"That was my first thought, but then I gave it a second thought. That tunnel and room may or may not contain the Miller treasure. Also, there's no way to know if Gramps ever found it, or even if he knew of its existence. We have four others depending on us to stay focused. The Miller treasure is our backup plan if the first one fails."

"Okay, that makes sense."

"Besides, there's another reason to be here."

"And that is?"

"The town needs a new library. We've got one to share, but it's not ready. We have to finish clearing it and the path to and from the door. We can rope off the rest of the rooms until we're ready to open the museum."

Mara sank gracefully into a chair facing him. He hadn't looked up from the book in his hands, but he wasn't turning any pages. "Jace?"

"I promised it to you, Mara. I intend to keep that promise."

"I know," she replied softly, as she reached for his hands, "and I trust that, but shouldn't we focus on the quest first?"

"I suppose," he replied, squeezing her fingers gently. "Maybe we can do both. We have to fix up the library and I'm still convinced we'll find something in here."

"Then let's get to work," she smiled, giving his hand one last squeeze before taking out her notebooks and getting started.

"Mara, did that investigator give you any idea why he was accusing you?"

"The fire started in the archives," she sighed in reply. "It's common knowledge I've spent a lot of time in there lately."

"Moron," he grumbled.

"That's what Morgan called him," she giggled.

"Good."

"Thanks for sending him packing, by the way."

"All my pleasure. He was looking for a way out of paying the policy. I just made it plain to him that he needed to look elsewhere. Pursuing his original line of thought would end up costing him his career. Investigative supervisors don't like to hear the word lawyer unless they have a solid case. He didn't and to push could cost him his job."

"You used to do that kind of work?"

"Yes, and I'm not overly proud of a lot of things that job demanded of me. I intend to spend the rest of my life trying to balance the scales."

"What made you decide that?"

"A beautiful woman told me a story," he replied, as he gazed into her eyes. "In that story I saw what I might have become, and it scared me. I don't want to be that, and I know I could never be worthy of her if I became that. I want to be worthy of that woman, and I want to make sure all trace of Gramps' influence is gone from my life. I want to be the good guy for a change."

"You are a good guy, Jace Harper, make no mistake there. And you're certainly worthy of the woman, you are. Just look at those two sleeping puppies there. Both would be dead if you hadn't taken them on."

"They're such loving creatures," he said, as he reached down to scratch a floppy ear. "I'm starting to see what Morgan meant. He said to watch the dogs to learn how to love unconditionally, to learn what true loyalty means. I think I get it. It's not about me and what I need; it's about them and what they need. It's about the woman I love and what she needs. That's how these guys function and I plan to practice that every day."

"So, just who is this lucky woman?" She was smiling cutely at him, and he lost all sense of time as he got lost in those eyes.

"Her name's Mara," he managed after a moment, "and she's the most amazing woman ever."

"Really? So how do you plan to approach her?"

"I'm going to take her sister's advice and try flattery. What do you think? Will it work?"

"All too well," she laughed. "All too well, Sir."

"Good, then I'm on the right track," he grinned.

They worked quietly but efficiently, chatting easily about the few things they found pressed between the pages. Mara made notes of the books with pages turned down for future reference. Darkness fell and Jace ordered pizza and soft drinks to be delivered. They broke for the meal, fed the dogs the scraps of crust, and then went back to work. It was getting late when a book slipped from Mara's hand and hit the table.

"Oh," she startled, and snapped it up again.

"You're falling asleep," smiled Jace. "I think we've done enough for today. Shall I walk you home?"

"You could take me home," she replied.

"No, I hate sleeping on the couch," he grinned. "You've still got some residuals from the hangover. I'll take you to your apartment then go back to the cottage and lament my stupidity for turning you down."

He was standing and holding out a hand to her. She took his hand and he helped her to rise. Mara stepped into his arms and nestled her head against his chest, inhaling the scent of him and getting lost in it. His arms enfolded her gently and he kissed the top of her head. "I've been sending you mixed signals, haven't I?" she said.

"You're making me crazy, Mara," he replied, "but then, that's what women do, isn't it? You drive men crazy, right?"

"Sorry, but it's in the Big Girl's Handbook. You have to drive the guy nuts to make sure he wants and needs you," she giggled.

"I thought as much," he chuckled in reply.

"Is it working?"

"All too well," he sighed, kissing the top of her head again.

"I'm so sorry, Jace. I really am. I'm just so confused and afraid."

"Afraid I'll turn out like all the other guys?"

"Sorry."

"Don't be; it's only natural. You've been hurt before and don't want to repeat the experience."

"But it isn't fair to you, Jace. I said I wanted to go slow, then tried to drag you into bed. I couldn't blame you if you took me up on it then tossed me aside for being too easy."

"That'll never happen, Mara. I don't think you're easy, just the opposite. I think you're very special. I also think you're conflicted between past experiences and what could be if this thing is right and real. Mara, I want you, but I want all of you, not just a fast roll in the sheets, as nice as that would be. It'll make me completely nuts, but I'm willing to wait until you're sure and ready."

"It's not fair, Jace Harper," she said, as she lightly pounded his chest with her fist. "You're supposed to be all over me, and I'm supposed to be fighting you off. I'm supposed to be the sensible one. It's not fair what you do to me."

"Do I make you crazy?"

"Yes, you do, dammit."

"Good. Misery loves company, so..." He got no further as Scoot began to whine and do the pee pee dance.

"All right, all right, we're coming," called Mara. "Scoot, your timing is terrible." She opened the door and both dogs raced out to do their business. Mara followed and Jace cut the power to the house before he came out and locked up.

"Jace, the outside light just went out," she said, as he joined her on the steps.

"I know. I cut the power. I don't want Gramps burning down this place too. We have to find that map and clue. We have to put this old bugger out of commission. It's the only way you and I will ever be able to relax and enjoy life."

"But what about the burglars?"

"Oh them, I gave one a key and the boys will warn me if the other one is around."

"Beast," she said, as she slapped his arm. He chuckled and when he smiled at her, she felt a tingle deep in her belly.

"Come on, pretty lady, let's go put the boys in the cottage then I'll drive you home."

She took his hand and they wandered slowly back to the cottage. He put the dogs inside, then drove her back to her apartment building. Mara leaned across the car and kissed him soundly. "Jace, thank you for everything, especially for being so understanding and gentle with me."

"All my pleasure, Mara."

"Meet me for breakfast tomorrow at the café?"

"Shall I pick you up?"

"Perfect. See you at eight." She kissed him again, then bolted from the car before she lost her resolve. Jace watched until she was safely inside the building then he drove home.

The dogs kicked up a fuss when they heard the car, but stopped when he called out to them. "It's just me, guys. Dad's home, all's well." They met him at the door with wagging tails and slobbery kisses.

"I love you both, yes I do," he said, as he wrestled with the dogs, "but Mara is a much better kisser than you guys. Yes, she is. I know, I know, I want to bring her home with us too, but not yet. She's not ready yet. No, she's not. I'm going to wear out my left hand before this gets settled, yes I am." The dogs had no idea what he was saying, but they were enjoying the play time.

"I thought I heard you come in," smiled Meghan, as she appeared at Mara's door. "Not staying with Jace tonight?"

"No," replied Mara, as she kicked off her shoes and flopped into her easy chair. "What about you? Has Ira gone back?"

"Yes, he left this morning and I'm lonesome already."

"Love at first sight? Meg?"

Meghan stretched her long form out on the sofa and smiled dreamily. "I know, I know, it's a disaster waiting to happen, but it is what it is. That mountain of muscle is just so delicious, don't you think?"

"He's a hunk all right, and he's sure all gooey over you. Did you guys talk at all, or did you just have sex?"

"That's the weird part, Sis. We didn't have sex. I knew we both wanted to, but we just talked instead. That was the scary and thrilling part of it all, Mara. He's a pretty boy and we both wanted each other, but he wanted to talk to me too. That was a strange thrill in itself; that beautiful hunk of man wanted to talk to me. He actually listened when I spoke. We got completely lost in conversation while he was here.

"That's never happened before, and it got to me. I was all ready to go into this physically first, you know, to get the sex out of the way and to see if there was anything more there after the heat died down a bit. Ira had other ideas. He wanted to talk to me, to find out all about me. He wanted to know what I thought about a dozen different things. Mara, that was a real thrill."

"Oh, girl, it sounds like you've got it bad for the big boy."

Meghan laughed at that. "Oh, you could tell?"

"Oh yeah, I could tell," smiled Mara. "I'm an Irish witch too, and I can see right through you."

"So what about you and Jace? What's going on there?"

Mara sighed deeply and though for a moment before she replied. "I nearly blew it, Meg. I think this guy is for real and I started to treat him like he was just like the others."

"What happened?"

"Oh, we got all hot and heavy then I backed off and told him I wanted more than a romp in the sheets. He agreed to go slow and was okay with it. That was working well until the damned library caught fire."

"Oh?"

"I left his place and went down there. God, all my efforts, years of work, and it was all such a complete mess, books, papers, magazines, walls and wood all burned and mixed with the water they sprayed on it to put out the fire.

"I came unglued and went back to Jace for comfort. I asked for a sip of wine while I sobbed out my soul on his shoulder. That beast kept refilling my glass until I was loaded.

"Uh oh, then he tossed you in the bed?"

"Yeah, but he just tucked me in and slept on the couch. I tried to drag him in with me, but he wouldn't. He said not until I was sober and had three days to let the hangover go away completely."

"Oh my god, a real gentleman with scruples in this day and age? Oh Mara, you have got to find a way to keep him."

"Working on it, Sis, working on it. Anyway, he said he knows I'm conflicted because of past experiences and he's willing to wait until I sort myself out."

"Well start sorting, woman. You don't want this one to get away."

"Dammit, Meg, what happened? I had my world completely under control, had sworn off men, and had found peace in my own company. I stopped dieting and enjoyed the few extra pounds that good living put on me. Everything was perfect, and then Jace Harper moved into town. What the hell happened?"

"Hormones dear," giggled Meghan. "Hormones and a ticking biological clock. It's not your fault; it's engineered into all of us. The right one for natural breeding walks into a room and all common sense flies out the window."

"Yeah, so, is that what happened to you?"

"No, I started hearing voices and went crazy enough to listen to them. Next thing you know the man of my dreams walks in the door and my good sense walked out. The rest you know.

"So, change of subject now; Ira says you're helping them with the quest."

"Yes. He told you about that?"

"He did. Man, that grandfather of theirs was a real piece of work."

"Yes, he was. All right, since he confided in you, we can discuss this openly now. Let me tell you how I think all this got started and what it's all about." Meghan listened intently as Mara told her what she'd told Jace.

"So you think this old bastard's ghost has inhabited all the men down the line, including Ira's grandfather?"

"It's the only thing that makes sense, Meg."

"So the voice in our heads is the ghost of the witch? The one who was sold into marriage with him?"

"I believe that's true," replied Mara.

"Okay, I'm still with you. Does Ira know?"

"We haven't had a chance to share that with the others yet. I just sort of got it put together in my head after the meeting. Next meeting I'll explain it to the others."

"Can I tell Ira?"

"Sure, go ahead. I'll tell Morgan. He'll be in town for another day or so."

"Okay, I'm going up next week to spend a few days helping Ira search. I'll tell him then."

"Wow, you're not wasting any time, are you?"

"Mara, I have no idea what the hell is going on here, but I do know one thing. Ira feels right. I see his face smile at me when I walk into a room, and I feel like I'm home at last. I get sweet thrills and chills every time he touches me, but I feel safe with him, like I could just relax and let it all go and I'd still be safe."

"Yup, you've got it bad," giggled Mara, "but I know what you mean. Being held in Jace Harper's arms is my new safe haven. Nothing bad can ever happen to me there. I'm ashamed to admit how badly I want to be there forever."

"I hear that. You know, sis, I just had a thought. Maybe we haven't figured it all out just yet. Maybe the men aren't going to be able to find the treasure until they find love first. Do you think the witch wants them to find love like her younger sister did? Could the women be part of the puzzle?"

"Gods, I hadn't thought of that, but I'll bet you're right. She loved her sister, and it was evil and meanness that destroyed her. Maybe she does want love to avenge her. Remember what Grandma always used to say, the best revenge is living well. I think you're on to something here."

"Yeah, but we can't tell the guys this. At least not yet."

"Oh, hell no, a man would never understand that," giggled Mara. "But we will have to match up the others."

"I think the witch is way ahead of us on that one. So, what's your plan now that you're unemployed?"

"Live off what's left of my trust account and help Jace find the damned treasure. I think the real key to the whole thing is here in Higgston. This is where it all started and the Miller place was actually built by old Phidias Tomlinson. His grandson sold it and moved away, changing his name to Miller. Sometime later another Miller bought it back, his son sold it, then the boys' grandfather eventually bought it back, but only lived in it for a year or two before he left it empty. I'm convinced the key to the whole thing is here in Higgston."

"You could move in with Jace; you know, save the rent money," grinned Meghan.

"Don't tempt me," laughed Mara, "I just might do it."

First Piece of the Puzzle

Mara sat rubbing her neck, staring at the books on the table before her, when a coffee magically appeared at her elbow. She grasped Jace's hand and squeezed it tightly. "You're a mind reader, Jace. This is exactly what I need."

He brought his own mug and sat facing her. "Yeah, I figured. We're down to a half dozen bookcases, then the library's done. I'm starting to get nervous. It's been weeks and nobody has found..." his phone was buzzing urgently.

Jace reached over to where the machine was doing circles on the table and punched the speaker button. "Harper."

"Jace, Jace, it's Logan. I've got it!"

"Got what? The chicken pox or a bottle of brandy?"

"Neither, but I'm going for that brandy soon. I found the map."

"Seriously?"

"Well, actually I technically didn't find it myself, but I've got it."

"So who found it?"

"Jimmy did."

"Logan, who's Jimmy?" laughed Mara.

"Sorry, I'm so excited I'm not making sense. Jimmy is my girlfriend's nephew. Renee was babysitting today, and he wanted to see the haunted house, so we brought him up. He asked what we were looking for, so I told him.

"The kid is ten years old. He wanted to know who hid it, boy or girl. I said boy so he wanted the see the boy's room. I showed him the smaller bedrooms. Dang kid had the box in less than twenty minutes. It was behind a hidden panel at the back of the closet. The box contained a piece of a map and an envelope. The envelope had a short rhyme and a note addressed to me. The note said "Congratulations, Logan. Here's a bonus." There was another cheque for $250,000."

"Jesus, Logan, that's great news," said Jace. "Buy Jimmy something nice for his birthday."

"I did. All he wanted was a new game system, so I went out and bought it for him. His dad's setting it up now. So, anybody else check in?"

"Nope, you get first prize," laughed Mara. "Logan, thanks so much for calling. You've given us new hope."

"All my pleasure, folks. Gotta run. See you next week."

"Bye, Logan," they said in unison. Jace reached over and tapped the off button.

"You hear that, Gramps?" asked Jace. "That's just the first crack in the armor. The rest will come and you'll be toast." He sat back in his chair, lost in thought.

"Jace, what is it?"

"I'm trying to be the new me."

"Oh?"

"Yes. At first I was disappointed that I hadn't been first. I passed that off, then felt jealousy. I've come to the conclusion that those are traits of Gramps that I don't want. I want to be happy for Logan. How about we take the rest of the day off to celebrate his victory."

"That's a wonderful idea," she smiled. "What shall we do?"

"Let's pack a lunch then put the boys in the car and head out of town, find a walking trail where they can run loose for a while, and just watch them play. We can cuddle under a tree or something while they snuffle around and pee on everything."

"That's a wonderful idea," she smiled. "Let's do it."

They closed up the house and returned to the cottage where Mara made a lunch while Jace put an old blanket over the back seat of the car. He brought a huge thermos of water for the dogs and Mara added two root beers to the lunch for them.

They spent a pleasant afternoon strolling around the perimeter of an abandoned farm. The dogs were happily sleeping in the back of the car as Jace drove home. Mara reached over and squeezed his arm affectionately. "Jace thank you for this afternoon. It was loads of fun and just the break I needed."

"We both needed that," he smiled, as he patted her hand. She laced her fingers through his and they drove the rest of the way home linked together.

Jace pulled up and parked in front of the cottage, then let the dogs out of the back. To his surprise they both went on alert and fixed their gaze on the big house. "Something's going on up there," said Mara.

"Yes it is," he replied, as he started up the path. "Go get 'em, boys." The dogs needed no further urging. They raced on ahead.

Jace had installed a doggy door in the old kitchen so he wouldn't have to be the dogs' butler all the time. The two dogs blasted through their door and raced to the library. Jace and Mara heard a man's voice scream in terror. They hurried and found the big burglar standing on a table in the library. Billy had him cornered and was snarling, but not attacking. Scoot was right beside him.

"Well now," gloated Jace. "We've got you this time, you son of a bitch."

"Call off the fucking dogs."

"Oh, hell no," said Jace, "not until the police get here."

"No, no cops."

"Tell me what you're looking for."

"Old man Miller's journals," replied the man sourly, being careful to stay out of Billy's reach.

"What the hell makes you think Gramps kept a journal?"

"Not your grandfather, you moron, his father. Your grandfather was an imbecile."

"Can't argue that," replied Jace, as he put his foot up on a chair and leaned his elbows on his knee comfortably. "Keep talking."

"The old man was a miser and reputed to keep a journal of everything he acquired. He was supposed to have kept it here in the house."

"Okay, so far so good," said Jace, as he turned the chair around and sat straddling it, his arms folded across the back. Mara was leaning her hip against the table, her arms folded across her chest and frowning at the burglar. "Now, this place has been empty for years, why are you just getting around to checking it out now?"

"Because I only heard about all this a few months ago. This is what I do. I find old abandoned places and reap the treasure hidden inside. Nine out of ten times, the abandoned house yields nothing, but then you score."

"You ever consider getting a real job?"

"I had one, but some rich bastard like you outsourced it out to India."

"Now that I believe," sighed Jace. "All right, come down out of there. Here, Billy, come here boy." Reluctantly, the dog backed away until he was at Jace's side. Scoot was already between Mara and the stranger.

"Now listen carefully," Jace went on. "We've been all through this place with a fine-tooth comb. We didn't find any journals. If we had, would we still be playing around in this old library when Tahiti is calling? Take my word for it; this old place is a bust. My miserly old grandfather left me this place and not a damn thing else."

"Oh yeah? My research says he was richer than god."

"Maybe he was, but I sure didn't get it. What I got was this money pit. All right, you haven't stolen anything, and you haven't wrecked anything, so I'll let you go, but this is the last time. I find you here again, I'll let the dogs have you then call the cops to get what they leave."

The man had edged his way to the door then stopped and looked back. "You're a decent guy, Harper. I'll move on and let this go, but don't you give up. There's something here worth finding, I can feel it." With that he disappeared through the door and raced down the hill.

"That bugger should take up marathoning," growled Jace, as he watched him go. "For a big man, he's damned fast."

"Jace, you let him go?" asked Mara, as she stepped up beside him and hooked her arm through his.

"Ah, he didn't hurt anything, Mara, not really. He's had his ass kicked by the powers that be already and is just trying to stay afloat. I can understand that. Besides, he gave us new information and I don't think he's as smart as he thinks he is."

"Oh? What do you mean?"

"Okay, an old man, a miser is keeping journals of his treasures, where does he keep those books from prying eyes?"

"In a safe?"

"That's my guess. That next room was the old geezer's study. I'll bet there's a hidden wall safe in there somewhere."

"Want to go look for it?"

"Girl, you read my mind." He chuckled as he put his arm around her waist and pulled her close. "Let's take a break from the books and go treasure hunting." They found the safe when a book pulled from a nearby shelf triggered a sliding wall panel an hour later. Finding the combination would be another matter.

Another hour later, Jace was ready to give up. "It's no use, Mara, the old bugger probably kept the combination in his head. He wouldn't trust anyone with it, and he'd be too paranoid to write it down and hide it."

"Wait, I've got an idea," she said, as she pulled her phone from her pocket. Her fingers flew then she put it on speaker as it was ringing. A woman answered. "Hello, Aunt Louise, I need a favor."

"Sure, Mara, what do you need?"

"I need to borrow your safe cracking gadget."

"Whatever for?"

"We've found an old wall safe in the Miller place. We want to see if it has any treasure in it."

"All right," chuckled Louise. "I'm on my way out for bridge night. I'll put it on the kitchen table for you."

"Thanks, Auntie."

"No problem. Happy safe cracking."

"Give me fifteen minutes, Jace, and we'll have this baby open wide."

"So you're a safe cracker too? I suppose that's a natural for a burglar. I can see why you did it, Mara. After all you're just following the family tradition."

"Stop it," she laughed, as she slapped his arm. "Aunt Louise was a nurse. The old safe in the town library didn't always obey the combination exactly. She used to bring in her stethoscope to listen for the tumblers. Now you stay here and behave yourself while I go get the tools of the trade." She hurried out the door and down the hill.

"Aunt Louise must live close by," he mused. "She didn't take the car. Ah well, come on boys, time for a pee break." He went outside with the dogs to wait for her return.

Jace sat on the front porch watching the two dogs snuffle around, checking stuff out, tails slowly waving back and forth.

"A while ago you guys were on death row," he said, as they returned to make sure he was all right. "Now you act like you haven't a care in the world. Is that the big secret, you guys? Huh? Is that it? That was then and this is now. Today you're well fed, you have friends, people you love and can hang out with, a place to sleep tonight, and a meal to look forward to in the morning. Life is good, right? Life at this moment is perfect, is that it? Live in the moment and to hell with the rest?

"Yeah, I'll bet that's what Morgan was trying to get me to understand. Well guys, life for me right now is pretty darn good, too. Now if I could just figure out how to convince Mara I truly do love her; that would clinch it for me. To hell with all the rest. You guys are right, all you really need is a proper pack to love and enjoy, a full belly, and a warm place to sleep at night. Everything else isn't all that important, is it?

"Well, you two fur balls lucked out, didn't you? You've got each other and me for a pack and we'll add Mara as soon as we can. Yes, we will. We've got a place to get in out of the weather, and the larder is full. Everything is just about perfect."

"What's perfect?" asked Mara, as she came striding in the driveway, breathing deeply.

"You are," replied Jace, as he rose and took her in his arms. He turned and swept her into a deep dip and kissed her.

"Oh god," she breathed, as their lips slowly parted, "tell me what that was for so I can do it again."

"It's for being the most beautiful safe cracker in the world," grinned Jace.

"You're getting way too good at that flattery thing." She giggled as she kissed his cheek, then grabbed his hand and led him back inside to the study and the offending safe. It took her a few tries, but she finally got the old safe opened.

Inside they found what they expected, but were amazed at the sheer volume. There were four books in all, each completely filled with lists of items, diamonds, gold coins, etc. Each item was described and the name of the person he'd acquired it from was noted. Some even had a description of how he'd forced someone into a financial position where they'd had to part with the item.

Jace dropped one book on the old dusty desk and sighed deeply. "Run for your life, Mara."

"What? Jace, what's wrong?"

"I come from a long line of complete bastards. The chance of my turning out like one of these guys is pretty strong. I wouldn't want to saddle you with a life chained to a man like that."

"Hey, you know what, it's getting late and we haven't eaten a darn thing since lunch. I think you've got the low carb blues."

"What? Oh yeah, you could be right. Sorry. It's just that he seemed to enjoy crushing someone who owned something he wanted. That was as much fun for him as acquiring the object was."

"Come on," smiled Mara, as she put the books back in the safe and closed the door on them, "I'm taking you back to the cottage and making us something to eat. You've gotten all blue, and I won't have it. We've had a great day and made a big discovery."

"You're right, pretty lady. It's been a wonderful day and I won't get depressed over the misdeeds of my ancestors. I do need to eat, let's go."

Mara waited outside with the dogs while Jace closed up the house and turned off the electricity. They walked down the hill hand in hand. Mara set about preparing a meal while Jace watched her every move. "Like what you see?" she asked, when she caught him looking.

"I do indeed like what I see, pretty lady," he grinned, looking her over and licking his lips.

"Stop that," she laughed, "or you'll never get anything to eat."

"So, what are you making?"

"Breakfast," she replied. "Bacon, eggs, toast, and warm milk."

"Warm milk, not coffee?"

"Coffee at two a.m., Mr. Harper?"

"Warm milk sounds perfect, Miss O'Grady," he grinned.

Mara fussed about the kitchen for a few more minutes and then served up the meal. "Jace, is there anything about this evening that sends up a red flag for you?"

"You mean our suddenly getting a strong lead to old man Miller's treasure and no clue about the real quest?"

"Yes, that."

"Are you thinking Gramps has been messing with our burglar to keep our focus on him?"

"It crossed my mind," she smiled.

"Yeah, mine too. He's enough of a greedy crook for Gramps to have recognized a kindred soul all right. So what do you suggest, leaving that safe closed and getting back on track tomorrow?"

"Precisely. I love it when a man understands me."

"Now you're trying to frighten me."

"Is it working?"

"Yep. If word leaks out I can understand women, I'll lose my man card and every friend I ever had. That, or I'll be on the circus bill as a freak of nature."

"Well, we can't have that," she laughed. "I promise I won't tell a single soul."

"God bless you, Mara O'Grady, you're a good woman," grinned Jace. The sweet interlude ended as Mara's phone began to ring. She dashed to her purse and grabbed it.

"Mara. What??? Okay, slow down honey, I'm already on the road." She clicked off the phone and stepped into her shoes. "I have to go, Jace. One of Arlene's girls is violently ill and she needs to get her to the hospital." She pulled on her coat, kissed his cheek, and then bolted for her car. He stood in the doorway, watching as she sped away.

As Mara disappeared around the bend in the road Jace turned toward the dark and silent house on the hill. "If you've started fucking with the kids now, Gramps, the gloves will come off and damned fast. Tell me even you can't be that low." He got no answer, just a feeling of foreboding. He went back inside and cleaned up from the meal.

Just as he was finishing up, his phone rang. "Harper."

"Jace, it's Mara, everything's okay. It was her appendix, and we got her here in time. Arlene is staying with her. I'm taking Elisa home and staying there with her."

"Get some sleep, sweetheart. Take care of yourself."

"You too, Jace. I'll call tomorrow with an update. Good night, dream of me."

"I will, I promise." Jace Harper was smiling as he tossed aside his phone and headed for bed, Billy and Scoot trailing close behind.

Busy Days

Mara awoke on Arlene's sofa, Elisa snuggled in her arms and sleeping soundly. She rose carefully and carried the girl back to her bed, tucked her in, and then lay down beside her. "Sweet thing," she smiled, as the child cuddled closer. "I hope I have a girl as sweet as you one day. What do you think, Jace Harper? Could you help me make a pretty little girl? Oh god, Meg's right, my biological clock must be ticking; that's why I'm getting broody. Go to sleep, Mara, O'Grady, go to sleep." She closed her eyes and drifted off again.

Jace awakened after only a few hours of sleep. Billy was doing the pee-pee dance, and both dogs wanted their breakfast. "It's all very fine for you guys," grumbled Jace, as he fed them. "You get to sleep most of the day anyway. There, are you happy now? Fine, then I'm going back to bed." Both dogs were face down in their food bowls. They ignored him until the food was gone then they followed him to the bedroom.

The ringing phone brought him around again at noon. "Harper," he yawned, as he thumbed the phone to life.

"Hi, Jace, it's Mara."

"Any news?"

"Little Jamie is doing fine but will be in hospital for a few days. Meghan is running the café for now and Morgan is helping."

"Morgan's back in town?"

"He calls Arlene every morning to say hi. When he found out what had happened, he hit the road for Higgston. I thought he was dangerous at first, but I'm starting to like Morgan Ross more and more all the time."

"Yeah, I think Morgan is sort of like Billy and Scoot, dangerous if provoked, but it's not his nature, really."

"Jace, it might be a few days before I can get back to the library."

"I understand. You take care of family, and we'll get back to the quest when everything settles down again."

"Jace, you don't have to put everything on hold just for me, you can…"

"Silly woman, this is a joint project, and it'll wait until you're ready to continue. In the mean time I'll find ways to entertain myself."

"Darn, I was hoping you'd just sit at home and pine away for me," she giggled.

"Of course I'll pine away for you. You're all I ever think about when you're not here. You're my whole world."

"Oh, Jace, that was wonderful. You're really getting good at the flattery thing."

"Thanks. Is it working?"

"It's starting to."

"I guess I'll just have to keep it up," he grinned. "Will I see you later?"

"I'm not sure. I'll call and let you know when I have more information."

Jace took a different tack that afternoon. He explored the basement of the house, but found nothing. Finally, he returned to the study where the safe was behind the hidden wall panel. He sat in the cracked leather chair behind the desk and considered. "All right, this was the old bugger's private study. He had his safe in here. I'll bet the entrance to his passageway is here, too. Now where would it be?"

Jace started to rise to inspect the walls, then he sat back down. "I wonder, might the trick be right here in his desk?" He began to explore the desk carefully. The drawers revealed nothing special but as he reached under the desk top, he hit pay dirt. Three switches met his questing finger tips. The first one popped open the panel with the safe. The second one didn't seem to do anything at all, and the third popped open another wall panel.

Jace rose and reached the new discovery in two strides. At his touch, the panel slid back to reveal a hidden staircase. "Well, now, there we go. Okay, boys, let's go back and get a flashlight." The dogs followed happily; after all, a walk is a walk. They fetched the light, then he admonished them to wait in the study while he investigated the hidden passageway.

Jace stepped carefully into the opening. It was a passageway that ran along the wall for several feet then became stairs leading down. The air in the passageway was musty and damp and the steps were a bit rickety. He proceeded carefully until he reached the bottom. "Well I'll be damned," he muttered, as he swept the beam of light all around, "the old place has a full basement after all."

In his first inspection of the house he'd been surprised to see it only had a half basement. Now he could see the rest of the space. There were steps leading up in three different places. He could see his own tracks coming down one, so he knew where it went. He began to climb another. It went up and up then leveled off.

Jace could see light filtering into the corridor and stopped to see what it meant. It was a peek hole into one of the bedrooms. There were more. From this hidden corridor Jace could see into every bedroom as well as the large upper bathroom. "Why that dirty minded old bastard," he muttered. He continued along to the end and found another sliding panel that led into the master bedroom.

After a quick look he turned back along the passageway until he was back in the basement room. The third set of stairs led to viewing holes to most of the downstairs rooms. Once again he retraced his steps until he was back in the room. He paused again then began a careful inspection of the room itself. One hidden panel could easily reveal another passageway. It had grown dark outside before he found it. The panel slid aside and he grinned. Then the flashlight died.

Cursing like a madman, Jace felt his way along until he found what he believed to the stairs to the study. He was wrong. He realized his mistake when he had climbed too high. Backing down the steps, Jace lost his footing and fell. He cried out in surprise when his foot slipped, then his head struck a beam, and he knew nothing more for a while.

MORGAN ROSS STARTLED as the buzzing of the phone in his pocket jerked him to reality. The café was quiet and he'd been daydreaming in a chair, gazing out the window and dreaming of a different life.

"Morgan."

"Morgan, it's Mara. Jace isn't answering the phone and I'm getting concerned."

"You two have a spat?"

"No, it's not like that at all."

"All right, did you check the cottage? Maybe his battery is dead."

"No, I haven't. I'm still with Elisa and she's sleeping. Would you..."

"On my way, girl. I'll check in as soon as I find him."

"Thanks, Morgan. I wouldn't ask, but I'm really getting worried."

Morgan stood and took off his apron then reached for his hat. "That was Mara," he said, as Meghan raised an eyebrow at him, "Jace isn't picking up so I'm going to go check it out. Will you be okay here for a while?"

"Go. I'm good here, Morgan."

When Morgan reached the cottage there weren't any lights on. There weren't any at the big house either. He knocked but got no answer, and no dogs barked. Now Morgan was concerned. He whistled for the dogs and heard them barking from the big house. He ran.

Scoot met Morgan halfway to the house. He was barking excitedly and running back up the hill, urging Morgan to hurry. He reached the door and found it unlocked. Stepping inside he began to flick on the lights. Scoot was still trying to lead him somewhere.

He followed the dog into the study and saw the opened panel with the safe and the other with a dark passageway. He could hear the other dog whining somewhere inside that darkness. Moran fished his keychain from his pocket and flicked on the small light he kept attached to it. He then followed the dog inside.

The stairs led down and Morgan had just reached the bottom when he heard a man groan. There, at the bottom of another set of stairs was Jace, trying to sit up and defend himself from Billy's licking tongue at the same time.

"Jesus, Jace, looks like you cracked yourself a good one. Can you stand?"

"Not sure. Think so, maybe."

"Let's give it a shot." Morgan helped him to his feet, but the wave of dizziness sent Jace reeling. Morgan caught him and steadied him until he was more stable on his feet. "All right, now let's get you upstairs where there's enough light to see what kind of damage you did to that thick head of yours."

With Morgan's help, Jace managed to climb the stairs back to the study where he collapsed into the desk chair. "Yep, looks like you took quite a wallop, cousin," rumbled Morgan. "I'll pack you off to the hospital where they can sew you back together again."

"Gotta shut down," muttered Jace, as he fumbled for and found the switches to close the hidden panels. "Lock up. Dogs."

"We'll take care of that," grinned Morgan. "First, we get you into the truck then I'll lock her up with the boys still inside. They can be the security system until we get back. Come on now, stay awake with me." He helped Jace to his feet and steadied him on the way to the truck. Once Jace was in the passenger's seat he went back and locked the doors, admonishing the dogs to keep the burglars away.

Jace had started to drift off, but jolted awake again as the truck started. Morgan kept talking to him all the way to the hospital. As he helped Jace through the emergency ward doors, a nurse spotted them and came running. Morgan let her take him, then stepped back outside and pulled out his phone.

"Mara."

"It's Morgan. Jace took a tumble down a set of stairs and cracked his melon good. I've got him at the hospital now. He'll be fine, Mara. He'll be just fine. Your instincts are good, girl. I'll let him know he owes you dinner."

"Oh dear god, Morgan, thank you."

"Jamie is probably sleeping by now, Mara. I'll see if I can collect Arlene and bring her home so you can come down here and babysit Jace."

"Oh, Morgan, would you?"

"Working on it." The phone went dead and Mara sat back, trying to slow her racing heart. A short while later she heard his truck in the driveway.

Jace awakened slowly, the bright lights hurting his eyes. His head ached abysmally, and he fought a wave of nausea. "He's coming around," said a voice. "I'll give you a few minutes while I go check on another patient."

"Thank you, Doctor."

That voice. Jace knew that voice. Doctor? Right, Morgan. Morgan must have brought him to the hospital. Why was Mara here? Dammit, Morgan; there was no need to worry her.

"I'll kick his butt for this," he groaned, as he forced himself past the headache.

"Hey there, handsome. How're you feeling?"

"Like I've been hit by a truck."

"In that case, leave the butt kicking to me for a while. Whose butt do you want kicked anyway?"

"Morgan's."

"Morgan? Why? What did he do?"

"He didn't need to call and worry you. I'm fine."

"Morgan went looking for you because I made him do it. Of course he had to call me. I'll worry about you if I want to, Mister, and don't you forget it."

"Mara," he sighed, as he relented and let the headache win.

"Yes?"

"Thank you. I was in pretty bad shape when Morgan found me. How he found me is a real mystery."

"Scoot showed him where to look. Billy was trying to clean you up and bring you around. He wouldn't tell me where he found you, though. Why not? What were you up to, Jace Harper?"

As she talked softly, Mara was stroking his hand and soothing him. He could feel her affection for him in her tenderness and hear it in her voice. For the first time, he let the L word enter his thoughts. He was indeed in love with Mara, but this was not the time to tell her. Save that for another time when he was feeling better.

"I was exploring," he replied, as he gently squeezed her hand.

"You found the tunnel?"

"No, but I did find something else, more disgusting."

"Disgusting? Do tell."

"Save your disgusting conversations for later," smiled a small Asian woman with a stethoscope hanging around her neck. "Hello again, Mr. Harper. I'm Dr. Lee. That was a nasty concussion you had there. Let me have a look at you now." She began to inspect his head, checked his neck then turned her attention to the monitors she had attached to him.

"Well, Humpty Dumpty, we seem to have put you back together again. You need to take it easy for a few days, but you should be fine. I've seen lots worse."

"Oh yeah?" grinned Jace. The woman's good cheer was infectious.

"Yep, my dad used to coach minor hockey. Now, those guys really know how to crack a skull." She turned to Mara. "You can take him home now, but stay with him and keep an eye out. If he sleeps too much or if he displays any other unusual symptoms, bring him right back to me."

"Got it, Judy. Thanks for patching up my guy."

"All my pleasure, Mara," she smiled, as she hurried away on another errand.

"Judy?"

"Judy Lee and I went to school together. She's a real bubble of happy all the time; perfect personality for a doctor."

"Can't argue that," agreed Jace, as he struggled to sit up. Mara helped him and steadied him while he caught his balance. "Can you explain why, when it was my head that got injured, they took my pants?"

"Oh, well, you understand women; when we have a handsome man helpless we have to check him out, right?"

"Of course. How silly of me to forget."

She giggled at that. "Let me help." Mara held his jeans open then, as he put his feet in she eased them up his legs. She started to snicker.

"What's so damn funny?"

"It just occurred to me I've been trying to get these off you for weeks now and here I am putting them back on you."

"One of life's little ironies?" Jace was grinning now as she put his socks on him then helped him into his shoes. Getting the T-shirt over his head was a bit of a struggle, but they managed.

"Button downs for you for a while sir," she mused, as she took his arm to steady him on the way out.

"Yes, dear, and a hat."

"A hat?"

"They shaved half my head, didn't they?"

"Yes, they did, but it'll grow back."

"I just hope my skull does."

"Do you need more pain killers before we leave?"

"No, I'm just whining. Take me home, Mara."

"Oh now, that's the best offer I've had all day," she grinned.

"You've had other offers? Should I be jealous?"

"No, I haven't and yes, you should," she grinned. "Okay, here's the car. Easy now, don't hit your head as you get in." She settled him in the passenger's seat and got behind the wheel.

"So, now can you tell me what happened?" she asked, as they left the parking lot of the hospital.

"I found another hidden panel in the study. I thought it might lead to the tunnel, so I went for a flashlight and started exploring. I didn't find the tunnel, but I found a room with several sets of stairs leading out. There are passageways all through the house. Worse, they all have peep holes into all the rooms, bedrooms, bathrooms, etc. Bunch of sick bastards, my ancestors.

"Anyway, it's dark as Hades in there and my flashlight failed. I thought I had found the right steps to get out again, but I was wrong. I slipped, hit my head and fell. I vaguely remember one of the dogs trying to wake me. Suddenly Morgan was there, and then I woke up in hospital with an angel by the bed."

"Still working the flattery angle?"

"Hard as I can; is it working?"

"Perfectly," she smiled, as she pulled up at the cottage. "You can practice more once I get you inside and start making coffee."

"Coffee? Are you crazy woman? I've haven't hardly slept for days and you want to give me coffee?"

"Judy said to keep you awake for a while until your eyes clear up and the headache goes away. Doctor's orders." She was helping him out of the car as she spoke.

Suddenly there was barking from the house on the hill, and then both dogs came racing down to the cottage. They jumped up at Jace, tails wagging furiously, and then they began to snuffle him all over to satisfy themselves he was all right. "It's okay, boys, it's okay," he soothed, as he hugged them and scratched them behind the ears. "You guys did a great job. You found Morgan and showed him where I was. I think you both deserve a biscuit for that one. Right, Mara?"

"Absolutely," she grinned, as her questing fingers found the spare door key under the welcome mat. She opened the door and led them all inside, keeping the lights low so as not to hurt his eyes. She sat him in a kitchen chair where he could watch her make the coffee.

"Mara O'Grady, you're amazing," he smiled, as he watched her dancing about the small kitchen.

"Oh really? Please do tell me more," she smiled.

"No, seriously. I'd have been in bad shape by now if you hadn't sent Morgan looking for me. Now here you are, still taking care of me."

"I care about you, Jace Harper," she said, as she gave him her full attention. "Is that so hard to see?"

"I guess I just didn't recognize it, Mara. That's all. Oh, I've had girlfriends before, but it was more of a hormone thing for both of us. I truly doubt if any of them would have done what you did just because I wasn't answering the phone."

"That's so sad for them," she replied, as she set toast, peanut butter, and jam before him then brought coffee for them both.

"It's hard though, isn't it?" he mused, as he waited for her to sit before he began to butter the toast.

"What is?"

"Keeping the lust under control while you wait to see if there are any real feelings there."

"Yes it is, Jace. Is that what you're doing too?"

"Yeah. When you said you wanted to go slow, I decided I wanted that too. I wanted to know for sure you actually cared for me as a person. I know, I know, now I'm sounding like a girl. Please don't tell the guys."

"Mum's the word," she chuckled. "I do care about you, Jace Harper. You're a very special man."

"Thank you, Mara. You Irish are really good at the flattery thing."

She laughed and playfully slapped his arm. "So, now you've got some toast in you, are you feeling better?"

"Somewhat, why do you ask?"

"I want to do something special, something, defiant, and something romantic."

"Sounds like fun; what do you have in mind, pretty lady?"

"I want us to take our coffee and the dogs up the hill. I want to sit on that front porch with you and watch the sunrise. I want us to show Gramps that he failed again and that we, as a pack of dogs and humans are stronger than he is."

"I really like that plan," smiled Jace.

"Then, let's go; it's almost dawn. I'll put more coffee in that thermos and we'll go up."

While Mara got the thermos ready Jace found a blanket for them to wrap up in. He also put a few extra dog biscuits in his pocket for the boys. They walked up the hill together, the humans holding hands and the dogs snuffling about in the grass, tails up and wagging slowly.

They settled in on the porch just as the sun began to peek over the hill across the valley. It would hit them well before it graced the town nestled below. Jace pulled the blanket around them as he pulled Mara tight to his side. Smiling, she came willingly and laid her head on his chest.

She felt the light kiss on her hair before he spoke again. "Mara?'

"Yes, Jace?"

"You smell good."

"Thank you," she giggled.

"Mara?"

"Yeah?"

"You feel good in my arms."

"I like being in your arms. It's nice here."

"You could stay there forever if you want."

"Speak the words, Jace," she smiled softly. "I promise it won't hurt."

He chuckled at that. "Mara, I love you and want you in my arms forever."

"Oh, Jace, that was beautiful. It wasn't so hard, now was it?"

"Scariest thing I've ever done," he replied, "because either way around it changes things between us forever."

"Yes, it does, Jace."

"Mara?"

"Yes, I do love you too, silly man," she replied, as she raised her lips for a kiss. The kiss wasn't filled with passion and hunger as had their other kisses before. This kiss was soft, sweet, and filled with something gentler, brighter, and more loving.

"Oh gods, Mara," he breathed, as their lips parted and he hugged her tightly to him. "I don't ever want to let you go."

"You don't have to, Jace."

"I want to keep you forever."

"Was that a proposal?" she giggled.

"It was."

"Then, yes, silly man."

"Mara, I'm sorry if this was all sort of, dispassionate."

"No at all. I'm a librarian; I like things quiet and orderly."

"You're teasing."

"Yes, I am. Jace, were you serious?"

"Utterly. Were you?"

"Completely. Want to set a date?"

"How about the day after we solve this damn quest? I won't have you married to a beggar."

"You're not a beggar, silly, and you won't be, not ever. We'll solve it long before the money runs out, and if we don't we still have the Miller treasure for a backup plan. Even if that fails we'll be fine; I just know it. Please don't fret about the support thing. The day after we solve it, it is."

"Mara, do you remember our first kiss?"

"Oh do I, it's fueled my fantasies many times since that night. I really wanted you to tear off my clothes and jump my bones right there."

"Funny, that wasn't on my mind at all."

"Liar," she laughed, as she hugged him tighter.

"Yeah, I sure was on fire for you that night," he sighed, as he returned the hug. "Do you think we could revisit that kiss one day soon?"

"I'd love nothing more," she sighed, as she snuggled deeper into his embrace, "but not until you're fully recovered. In the meantime I get to baby you, understand?"

"Yes, Ma'am," he sighed. They sat for a while longer, Jace holding her tightly and Mara content to be held. When the sun was fully up he spoke again. "Mara?"

"Hmmm?"

"Sun's up. Can I go to sleep now?"

"Let me see your eyes," she said, as she leaned away from him. His eyes were clear and twinkling with merriment. "All right, but this time you get the bed and I get the couch."

"Mara..."

"Jace, please let me care for you."

"I was going to say, I love you."

"Sure you were," she giggled, as she gently poked him in the ribs. He winced and she was instantly contrite. "You poor soul, more than your head got hurt, didn't it?"

"Yeah, I thought I was near the top of the stairs, but Morgan found me at the bottom. I guess I'm pretty beat up."

"Then we'll save that ravishing for another day." She tucked herself under his arm so he could lean on her while they walked back to the cottage.

Once they arrived she shooed him off to the bathroom while she fed the dogs. When he returned she tucked him into bed where he melted into the cool sheets. "Sleep well and heal, Jace Harper, my love," she whispered, as she kissed his cheek and slipped out of the room. Jace smiled to himself as he heard her on the phone arranging for her Aunt Louise to babysit Elisa and for Meghan to bring her a change of clothes for later. Jace fell asleep to the sound of that magical voice in the distance.

Breathing Room

As Jace slept, he dreamed again of the evil man who haunted and hunted him. This time it was different. This time the man faced him, rage clear on his face, but he couldn't reach Jace who was holding Mara tightly, protecting her. A woman stood between Jace and the tormentor.

"It's done, Phidias," said the woman, "they survived and have united. You're beaten, you cannot have them."

"Pah, stand aside, woman, or I'll teach you your place." He tried to brush her aside, but the woman swept him back. He was startled at her strength. Fire danced from her fingertips and her hair blew back from her face, carried by a breeze only she could feel. Phidias seemed more frightened than angry now. "They have not yet consummated the union," he snarled. "There is still time."

"The love between them will keep you at bay and feed me strength," replied the woman. "Begone now, you cannot have them." Snarling Phidias faded away and the woman turned to smile at Jace and Mara. She blessed them then, she too, faded to leave Jace dreaming of holding Mara in his arms while they walked through a field of flowers accompanied by the two old dogs. Jace Harper slept peacefully for the first time in many days.

Awareness came slowly back to Jace, and he fought it. His dreams were sweet, and awareness brought pain. He groaned as he finally gave up and opened his eyes. Both dogs were instantly on their feet at his bedside, tails wagging. Jace groaned again as he sat up. Mara was quickly at his side, helping him to stand.

"How are you feeling, sweetheart?" she asked, searching his eyes. She smiled to see his eyes were clear.

"I feel like I went ten rounds with Morgan," he grimaced, as he tried to stretch out the kinks.

"That bad, huh?" she chuckled. "Can you make it to the bathroom on your own?"

"Sure."

"Okay, then I'll go fix you some breakfast."

"What time is it, Mara?" he asked, as he made his way slowly towards the target, leaning his hand against the wall for support.

"It's six p.m.," she called from the kitchen.

The face in the mirror made him grimace. They'd shaved a path right down the middle of his hair like a reverse mohawk. To make it worse, he had two days of scruff on his cheeks. "All right, time for a change." He sighed as he reached for his electric razor and flipped open the trimmer.

Mara heard the razor buzzing for a long while. "Wow, sure taking his time with that shave," she mused. Mara almost shrieked as she saw him. He'd shaved his head and trimmed his beard to a small goatee and moustache.

Jace emerged from the bathroom and made his way to a chair at the kitchen table. The place smelled wonderful. A plate of food and a tall mug of coffee later, he was feeling much better. "Edgy new look," she grinned, as he surfaced from his plate.

"I had to do something," he sighed. "I wasn't going out in public with a reverse mohawk."

"You are planning to grow it back, aren't you?"

"Just as soon as I get the stitches out of my skull, the hair comes back and the beard comes off."

"Glad to hear it. The tough guy look isn't one of my favorites."

"Mine either. Mara, I'm sorry; I didn't mean to sleep the day away."

"You needed to," said Mara. "We'll take it easy and put you to bed early tonight then we'll see how the world looks tomorrow."

"That works for me." He smiled as he reached for her hands. "Mara, I remember everything we said last night. I meant every word; I love you and want you beside me forever."

"I meant it too, Jace," she smiled. "I love you."

"You weren't sure I'd remember when I woke up, were you?"

"No," she blushed, as she lowered her gaze, "but I hoped you would."

He smiled and his eyes crinkled at the edges. Her belly gave a little flutter at that and she blushed. Damn, this man sure knew how to light her fire. "Mara, I know you've been hurt before. Someone made idle promises to you and didn't live up to them. I want to be the man who lives up to the standards you want and deserve. As badly as I want to, I won't ask you to move in with me until we're officially married."

"My god you're sweet, Jace Harper, but has it occurred to you I might want to?"

"Now there's the answer to my prayers," he grinned. "However, I want to talk about treasure."

"Treasure? Now?"

"Yep, now," he said, as he rose stiffly to his feet and fetched the coffee pot to refill their mugs. "Bear with me for a moment here."

"All right," she replied, as she stirred the cream into her coffee. "Tell me what's on your mind."

"I want to set aside the quest for a few days and go after the Miller treasure."

"Okay, why?"

"When we looked at those journals I saw a description of a diamond ring. He forced a man into bankruptcy to get it from the man's wife, but it's supposed to be in the collection."

"And?"

"And I want that ring for you. It's supposed to be one and a half carets and flawless, set in gold."

"Oh my god, Jace, I..."

"Don't get too excited, girl. First we have to find it."

"Oh, Jace, you're such a romantic; I love it. However, shouldn't we just redouble our efforts to finish our part of the quest? After all, the others are depending on us too."

"I've been thinking about that as well," he replied. "What say we share it with the others? We take out your ring then split the whole damn thing five ways even."

"Oh, Jace, that's a wonderful idea."

"It's still a gamble," he sighed, reaching for her hand again. "We might locate the place and find that someone has already cleaned it out."

"Oh I know, but wouldn't it be fun for us all to take a break from the quest and go on a treasure hunt together?"

"Okay, the next meeting is supposed to be a week Wednesday, how about I call the guys and let them know what we're up to."

"Shouldn't we keep it a secret until they're all here?" Just then they heard the growl of Morgan's truck outside. "Hush now; don't say a word," said Mara, a giggle in her voice. She rose and went to the door where she met Morgan and Meghan.

"I've brought you a few more clothes and essentials," said Meghan, "and Mother Hen wants to make sure Jace is going to live."

"Gotta keep the family healthy," rumbled Morgan, as he stepped past the girls and sat at the table facing Jace. "Look me in the eye and say *shit on a stick*."

"That's how I'm feeling," grinned Jace, "like shit on a stick."

"Good stuff," nodded Morgan. "Your eyes are clear, but I can see the pain. You took a long tumble. Pretty stiff and sore, right?"

"Right as rain. Morgan, thanks again for dragging my sorry ass out of there and getting me patched up."

"You'd do the same for me. Is there more coffee?" Morgan rose and poured a mug for himself. He also poured one for Meghan and filled Mara's mug before starting a new pot. Mara and Meghan were already sitting at the table as he returned. "Oh, love the new look, Jace."

"Right. Take a picture 'cause it won't last long." Morgan chuckled as he teased Jace, but watched carefully. Finally satisfied Jace was all right, he let it go.

"So, what's the big secret?" asked Meghan, as she took a sip of her coffee.

"What secret are you talking about Meg?" asked Mara.

"Don't play coy with me, sister mine. I'm an Irish witch and I can tell you're keeping something from me."

"So's Jace," grinned Morgan.

"Okay then, since the two of them are so damn smug, I'd say they finally hooked up," grinned Meghan. "Am I right?"

"In a manner of speaking," smiled Jace, as he reached for Mara's hand.

"Ah huh," said Meghan, "and what else?"

"What do you mean, what else?"

"You're still looking far too smug, Jace Harper," she replied. "Now cough it up or I'll put the hex on you."

"Mara, protect me," chuckled Jace.

"Oh go ahead, tell them, sweetheart," smiled Mara. "Meg won't give us a moment's peace until she gets it all."

"Count on it," grinned Meghan.

"All right, you savage," smiled Jace. "Mara and I have decided to put the quest on hold for a while and search for the Miller treasure."

"What??? Why?" demanded Meghan. "The other guys are counting on you too. You're not..."

"Easy, girl, easy," rumbled Morgan. "He's not finished yet, are you cousin?"

"Nope, there's more. We plan to split the treasure five ways, share it equally with the group. This way the pressure comes off the quest. I know I spent much of what I had to cover the back taxes on this place and I'm sure the same is true for the rest of the guys.

"We won't waste a lot of time on this, just a day or two, but I think we're pretty close already. Once everybody is here for the meeting we can all search together."

"You'd really split that with the rest of us, Jace?" asked Morgan. "It's not part of the original pact; that one's all yours."

"I don't know about you, Morgan," sighed Jace, "but I've grown to think of you guys as brothers instead of cousins. I never had much of a family, and I'm starting to enjoy having one. Yeah, we agreed to share the treasure and share alike, so I'm happy to throw this one into the pot too."

"You're a good man, Jace Harper, and I'll be proud to call you brother. I'm betting the more you learn about our ancestors the more determined you are to become the good guy."

"You know it," said Jace. "You too?"

"Yep," rumbled Morgan. "I've sworn off my evil ways and trying to balance the scales a bit. I'm betting the rest of the guys are, too."

"Ira sure is," Meghan said softly. "He told me the same thing."

MORNING CAME AND JACE found himself alone in the cottage. Mara's bedding was folded neatly and lying on the arm of the couch. He moved on to the kitchen where he noticed a note on the table.

"Jace, I didn't want to wake you. I have a few errands to run, and the larder is empty. I'll be back soon. Love, Mara."

He smiled and laid it carefully at his usual place at the table. He stepped to the counter and reached towards the coffee machine where he noticed another note. "Go ahead, push my buttons, you know you want to." Grinning, Jace peeked inside the machine. Yep, it was all primed; all he had to do was choose the strength and push the start button.

While the coffee machine did its thing, he poured himself a bowl of cereal and made toast. After he ate and was enjoying a coffee outside on the patio with the boys, he took out his phone and called Mara.

"Mara."

"Next time I start pushing your buttons I want you in the room with me."

She giggled at that. "So, how's the coffee?"

"Perfect, how are the errands coming?"

"Be home in a jiffy. Pour me up a mug and I'll be right there."

"Mara, are you on the phone while driving?"

"Hands free technology is a girl's best friend," she replied. "Start pouring."

"Yes ma'am, I hear and obey." Jace went back inside to pour her coffee and heard her car in the driveway. He went out to help her carry the bags.

"Could you bring in the two travel bags, please," she asked, as she laced her fingers through the handles of several plastic grocery bags. He scooped up the two suitcases, closed the back of the car and followed her inside. "Just drop them by the laundry machines, Jace," she called from the kitchen.

"Oh gods, that's delicious," she moaned, as she took a long sip from the coffee mug. "First cup of the day is always the best."

"First cup? You have been on the run."

"It's been a weird day and it's just getting started."

"What's going on, honey? You seem a bit agitated."

"Creeped out would be a better description," she sighed. "I started out to pick up a change of clothes and a few groceries. When I got to my apartment, I found someone had been going through my underwear."

"What???"

"Yep, some pervert has been into my panties."

"Did you call the police?"

"No. I know who did it."

"Okay, who was it and where do I find him?"

"Jace, don't go getting an assault charge. I'm moving in with Meg. She's moving back into Mom's house and I'll do the same."

"You could come here," he said.

Mara looked up to see the pleading in his eyes. In truth she wanted to, perhaps even more than he wanted it, but... "Soon, sweet man," she said, as she reached over to stroke his cheek. "We'll talk about just that very soon, I promise."

"Fair enough," he replied, as he kissed her fingers and released her hand. "So who was it?"

"Only two other people have keys to that apartment, Meghan and Mr. James."

"I am sooo going to kick his ass," growled Jace.

"No, Jace, let it go. Don't you see? This is just another one of Gramps' distractions. Mr. James is a grumpy old bugger, but he's been in that building for years and never did anything that would put the slightest mark on his record."

"Yeah, well, he must have wanted to for Gramps to be able to influence him."

"Maybe, but, but wanting to and doing are two different things. Just let it go. I'll be out of there quick as can be and I'll let him know why. He won't make a fuss."

"All right, Mara, I'll let it go for your sake."

Growing Closer

A while later, Jace was still fussing about Mr. James. Mara put her arms around him and hugged him tightly for a moment, then gently sat him back at the table and brought him coffee.

"Jace, this is Gramps' doing. It's a distraction; it means we're getting close. The best way to avenge this is to find the treasure, or at least our part of it. Once we have it in hand, he'll have to leave us alone."

"*There's another way.*"

He almost said it aloud, but he remained silent. If he told her about that dream she would never know for sure if it was for her or the treasure. Jace Harper wasn't about to give Mara any reason to doubt his love for her. He'd tell her after they were married, not before. "Okay, this is beginning to concern me," he said, as he took a sip from his mug.

"In what way?"

"In the amount of influence Gramps can exert on the solid world."

"All right, let's look at what we've got, regarding Gramps. We believe he started the fire at the library. He's tried to creep us out and whenever we start getting close something seems to happen to distract us, both from the quest and from each other."

"Agreed. I know this all sounds crazy, but I have no other way to explain any of it. I mean, I just put fresh batteries in that flashlight, yet it failed. Even then I should have been able to find the right set of steps. Now I'm suddenly talking about turning aside from the quest to chase another treasure. Mara, I'm starting to mistrust my own judgement here."

"Oh, really?" The expression on her face was easy to read and he was instantly contrite.

"Not you, silly woman," he smiled, as he reached across the table to take her hands in his. "My feelings for you are the one thing here I'm completely sure are my own. You said it yourself, every time we start to get close, something distracts us. He's not trying to put us together; he's trying to keep us apart."

"You're right, Jace," she sighed. "I'm sorry. So, why do you think he doesn't want us to get together?"

"There are two of them, ghosts, I mean. He's evil and tries to bring that to everyone he touches, right? She's opposing him, trying to help us send him to hell where he belongs. At least that's my impression of what's happening."

"So if greed, avarice, and the like are what he visits on everybody he touches, then is she bringing love to oppose him? Is she the one trying to put us together?"

"If evil makes him stronger, then it stands to reason that love would weaken him and make her stronger," mused Jace. "You said the woman told Meghan she'd meet the man of her dreams and not to waste time, right?"

"Yeah, that's right, and Morgan said he'd heard the voices. Oh, and Arlene just offered herself up to Morgan; she's never done anything like that at all before. All right, so the witch is trying to block him, and love is her weapon." She was thoughtful for a moment then spoke again.

"Dammit, now I'm doubting myself again. Is my hesitation with you my own or something Gramps has put in my mind?"

"I don't think he can, sweetheart. I think all he can do is amplify what's already there. You've been hurt before and are naturally a bit hesitant. You thought you were sure once before and it didn't work out. I think he can play on those fears, but nothing more.

"Actually, I think he blew it this time. By trying to knock my block off, he inadvertently brought us closer together."

"Oh my god, Jace, are you saying he tried to kill you?"

"I am, and I don't think it's the first time he's tried. Mara, what is it?"

"Oh, sorry, nothing really."

"Hey, bugger that, Mara O'Grady, talk to me."

"Jace, now I'm afraid that the feeling I have for you, the ones you have for me, aren't real. They could just be something put in our minds by the witch."

He took her hands and squeezed them gently. "Mara, I don't care at all if they are; I'm just enjoying the feelings."

"But what happens after the quest. Do we suddenly realize we made a mistake? When it stops, are we going to just go our separate ways?"

He smiled as he squeezed her fingers gently. "In order, Miss Librarian Mara: What happens after the quest, is we get married like we promised. This is no mistake, sweetheart. I don't ever want to have a day without you in it. Once I have you sewn to my hip I'll never let you go."

"Oh, Jace, I'm so confused. All this sounds crazy, and no one would ever believe any of it if we told them. I'm just so afraid that once we..."

"Sweetheart, the love will never stop. Stay with me now. The witch needs us completely besotted with each other. If we lose the love, Gramps could come back and she doesn't want that, so she will have to keep the mojo cooking."

Mara gazed into his eyes for a moment then let go of her fears. She replaced them with determination and love for this strange man who had suddenly appeared and turned her carefully constructed world on its edge. "All right, sweetheart. We want to be together, and if that's what is needed to keep him at bay then I'll move in here with you. By your reasoning, if we're together he can't get at us. You'll be safe and so will I."

"Mara, are you sure? It truly is what I want most in this world, to have you beside me always, but are you sure?"

"No, not really, but it's your job to allay my fears. Every day you stay with me will weaken the fears a bit more. They should disappear altogether in about a hundred years or so."

"Come here and let me hold you," he smiled, as he rose from the table and came to her. She stood and stepped into his arms. He hugged her tightly, whispering her name over and over. She melted as he kissed her, and then the fire lit in her belly. She pressed herself tightly to him, her leg hooking around his hips to pull him closer. His hand on the small of her back pulled her tighter to him as the kiss deepened. Then they heard the crunch of tires on the gravel driveway.

"Aw, god dammit it to hell," sighed Jace, "what now?"

"Don't worry, lover," giggled Mara, as she tried to straighten her clothes. "We'll revisit this again tonight, and we'll put the dogs on guard duty. Nothing will keep me from ravishing you next time."

"May the gods be good to me, for tonight my prayers will be answered."

"Hello the house," called Meghan's voice. "Anybody home?"

"No," replied Jace. "Go away, we don't want any. We gave at the office."

"Ira honey," laughed Meghan, as she opened the door, "I think we interrupted something."

"Meg, maybe we should come back later," replied Ira, staying outside, "like later tonight, maybe."

"Come on in, Ira," laughed Mara. "Are you here to help us move apartments?"

"I was summoned," he replied with a smile, "and so I came. Everybody loves Ira when it's moving day."

"I love Ira every day," smiled Meghan, as she kissed his cheek. "Is there coffee?"

"I'll put on a fresh pot," said Mara.

"So, what did we interrupt? Were you having sex?"

"Your timing is off," growled Jace. "You've about two minutes early."

"Oh, don't be a grumpy bear," grinned Meghan, as she gave him a little hug. "After all, the anticipation is half the fun."

"How would you know?" he groused.

"I'm an Irish witch and I know everything," she smiled, ignoring the barb.

"So what else do you know?"

"I know you two have to stop stalling and get it on before Gramps manages to kill one of you."

"What??? What are you babbling about, Meghan?" asked Mara, as she set the coffee pot to work.

"The evil spirit we call Gramps feeds off greed, fear, anger, and things like that. They make him strong. The spirit of the witch opposes him. Love feeds her and makes her stronger. You two are mad for each other. Get on with it and he can't touch you. As soon as you consummate the union he's helpless against you."

"Meghan, where the hell do you get this stuff from?" asked Mara.

"From the dreams," said Jace softly.

"So you had the dream too, did you?" asked Meghan.

"Explain please," said Mara, as she began to pour up coffee for everybody. Jace told her about the dream.

"I see," she said, as she sat to the table with the others. "You weren't going to mention this dream to me because it would just increase my doubts, right?"

"Busted," sighed Jace.

"When were you planning to tell me?"

"The day after we get married. That way there would be no doubts about my motives."

She reached out to lightly stroke his cheek with her fingers. "Sweet man, that just pushed aside all my doubts. Ira, I'll be moving in with Jace here at the cottage."

The rest of the day was spent in delightful activity. The men hustled all the heavy stuff, while the girls did the packing and unpacking. First they went to see Mr. James. Jace promised to behave, but Mara knew it was an idle promise. She hoped the superintendent wouldn't cause any trouble.

"What's going on?" asked Mr. James, as he opened his door to Jace's knock.

"Mara and Meghan will be moving out today," said Jace.

"What, now? They have to give a month's notice or lose their deposits."

"Listen carefully," said Jace, his voice cold and dangerous. "You were in Mara's apartment, you were going through her panties, and we can prove it. You go prepare a refund for both girls' deposits and nothing more gets said. You say a single word and we go to the police. Your call."

The man just turned red and nodded; his defeat was clear on his face. "I really don't know what came over me," he said. "It was like I was sleepwalking. I'll get the refund cheques ready; there'll be no arguments. Just leave the keys in the apartments and lock the doors as you leave. I'll take care of the cleaning."

"Thank you, that will be fine," said Mara coldly, as she started trying to pull Jace away. "Just put the cheques in the mail."

"To what address?"

"This one," replied Jace, as he passed Mr. James a business card. It had his name and a local post office box number.

The man nodded and retreated back inside his apartment. Before he could close the door Ira stopped him. "Hey buddy," he said, cracking his knuckles and flexing those monstrous muscles, "if I thought you'd been going through Meg's clothes, I'd be unhappy about that."

"I didn't," stammered Mr. James as he retreated and closed the door.

The process took much longer than they expected. First Ira and Jace rented a truck and loaded most of the furniture in it while the women packed boxes. Meghan went with them to direct the action as the furniture was placed in storage, then they returned. When they arrived back at the apartment house Mara was about ready. Her boxes were loaded in the truck and taken to Jace's cottage while Meghan finished her packing.

By the time Meghan had been moved out it was late, and they were all exhausted. They left the truck with Ira and Meghan to return in the morning. On their return to the cottage, they heard the dogs barking and whining. They were in distress. "Uh oh," sighed Jace, as he unlocked the door, "I think we might have been gone a bit too long."

The door opened and both dogs raced past him to the hedge, wasting no time in getting a leg in the air. The looks of relief on their faces made Mara laugh and promise them it would never happen again. Once the pressure was off the dogs returned, tails wagging furiously as they welcomed their humans home.

"It's funny, you know," Mara smiled wistfully. "I've lived in that apartment for a few years and thought of it as home."

"But?"

"But one look at that open dresser drawer and I knew it wasn't home. I felt wounded, violated, and vulnerable. I could never feel safe there again. I also find it a bit strange that my entire life can be jammed into a few cardboard boxes. It doesn't seem like much of a life, does it?"

"Your life isn't in these boxes, Mara," Jace said gently, as he took her in his arms. "That's just your stuff. Stuff comes and goes through the years of a life, but the life is what you've accomplished, learned, shared, experienced, and how you've touched the lives of others."

"That was beautiful, Jace. How did you get so wise?"

"I studied the How to be a Good Guy Handbook," he grinned. "There's lots of great stuff in there."

Mara giggled at that. "Well, I guess I should start unpacking."

"You can leave that for tomorrow if you like."

"No, I'll need fresh clothes tomorrow," she sighed. "I should unpack my clothes at least."

She stepped out of his arms and went to the bedroom where there were several boxes piled on the bed and her dresser from the apartment beside the old one he was using. Sliding open the closet doors she found it three quarters empty. "You're such a guy," she smiled.

"What?"

"Two pairs of jeans, one suit for weddings and funerals, and that's all you need. Ah well, lots of room for me." She popped open a box and began to unpack.

As Mara shook the wrinkles out of her clothes and hung them in her closet, she began to hum quietly to herself. She'd shake out a dress then hold it to her body and check herself in the mirror before hanging it in the closet.

Jace watched in fascination as her face registered each judgement of a garment's possibilities. There was more though; there was a growing lust in him as he watched her delicious curves moving with effortless grace through the room. The world around him retreated until there was only Mara and that sweet voice humming softly.

Slowly Mara became aware of the attention she was getting. With a shy smile and a soft blush she slowed down the process to give him a better show. A glance over her shoulder at the mirror showed the look of desire on his face and she felt a rising flutter in her belly. "*Oh yeah, now we're getting somewhere. Take a long look, Jace Harper.*"

Jace's mouth went dry as she kicked off her jeans and tossed aside her T-shirt. She slid a slinky dress over her head and adjusted it to show plenty of cleavage. She watched with delight as his Adam's apple bobbed when he swallowed hard, feasting his eyes.

"*Control it, Jace, control it; don't jump over the damned bed and rape her. Stay in control.*" He was doing fine until she whipped off the shirt and pulled on the dress. His jaw dropped and so did his control. Blood began to leave his brain and pool in his penis, which began to rise like a periscope, seeking the source of the pheromones that it sensed nearby.

Mara noticed the bulge in his jeans and groaned inwardly. Her body began to respond, preparing for the sweet primal act of union that was sure to happen this time. "*Oh my god,*" she thought, embarrassed. "*Surely he must smell my arousal. No, I will not rush this; I'll savor it.*"

"Mara," he breathed softly, but she pretended not to hear him. She slipped the dress over her head, shook it out and hung it in the closet, standing with her back to him, dressed in only her bra and panties. She swallowed hard this time and felt her body juices begin to flow faster. She could feel the moisture gathering in her panties and wanted to rip them off and jump on him.

She heard him move a step closer and caught her breath. Mara was almost a bit frightened now, but pushed that aside. Turning, she found him barely a pace away. Their eyes locked in a gaze of mutual desire and held for a long moment.

It took Jace a few moments to realize she had spoken. She'd asked him something. He struggled to understand. "The blue one," she whispered again, "pass me the blue one please."

With a visible effort he tore his eyes away from her delicious form and reached to pass her the blue dress. She held it up to her chin as she gazed in the mirror. She could feel his breath on her neck now and feel the heat of his gaze. "Mara."

As she turned slowly, the blue dress was taken from her and cast aside. She gasped softly as his hand found the small of her back and pulled her tightly to him. Mara groaned with delight and desire as his mouth found hers, hungry for her, needing her. The lump in his jeans pressed tightly to her belly and she began to fight with his belt.

"No," he panted, as he moved her hand away, "not yet. First I want my favorite fantasy."

"What???"

"Just be still and let me explore you," he breathed, as again his lips sought hers. She felt her bra come loose and get cast aside. She pushed and pulled at his T-shirt until it slid up enough for her to bury her bare nipples in the soft hair on his chest. She groaned with delight at the delicious tingle that sent through her entire body.

He reluctantly broke the kiss then gently pushed her back against the wall and began to sink to his knees, kissing and suckling at her nipples on the way down. "Jace, oh gods, what are you doing?" she moaned, as his lips traced their way down her belly.

"Wait a minute and I'll show you," he panted, as he hooked his fingers in the waistband of her panties and slid them down her legs. Jace inhaled deeply of the sweet aroma of aroused woman then began to nuzzle her thighs apart.

"I'll fall."

"I'll hold you up," he replied, as he nuzzled deeper between her legs, his lips and tongue searching and finding her core, his big hands gripping her buttocks.

"Oh my god," she groaned, as she grabbed his shaven head and pulled him closer, grinding her hips down on his hungry mouth. His lips and tongue played over all her delicate spots, driving her relentlessly toward a shattering orgasm. She cried out as it hit her, coursing through her with wave after wave of ecstasy. Her body convulsed and shook like the aftershocks of an earthquake as the bones turned to jelly and she melted towards the floor.

Jace rose to his feet with Mara in his arms. Turning towards the bed, he used his foot to push all the boxes off before he laid her gently on her back. "Don't go away; we're not finished yet."

"Speak for yourself, handsome," she purred, as he began to tear off his own clothes. She watched with rising interest as he became nude then climbed slowly onto the bed, hovering on hands and knees above her, breathing down at her like some primal beast. Swallowing hard, Mara gazed into his eyes. The burning lust she saw there both frightened and thrilled her.

"Come to me, Jace Harper," she breathed, as she reached to pull his head down for a kiss. As he lowered himself towards her she opened her legs and locked her ankles around his back. "I'm all yours, big fella, come take what you want."

"I want you, Mara O'Grady," he breathed, as his probing body found her entrance and slipped deeply inside her, bringing a groan of delight from her lips.

For a moment, Jace thought he heard a wail of frustrated rage and pain in the distance, but he ignored it as he thrust into her. As he began to move faster and faster he felt her delicate fingers slip between them. Mara was panting and groaning as was he, then his world exploded in stardust. He vaguely felt her finger move faster for a moment then she too groaned as her body convulsed once again.

Jace fell, more than rolled, aside and pulled her to him. "Mara?"

"Mmm?" she purred softly.

"You okay?"

"Oh yeah, I am so much more than okay," she sighed, as her fingers continued to trace circles through the hair on his chest. Are you...?"

"Ruined forever. You have to marry me now because after that no other woman could ever compare."

"I feel the same, my love; I feel the same." She continued to drift for a moment then was surprised to feel herself becoming aroused again. "Jace?"

"Yeah?"

"Do you think Uncle Wiggly here could be persuaded to try that again?" she asked mischievously, allowing her fingers to trace down his body until she grasped him tightly in her hand. "Oh my," she said with delight, "I do believe he likes me."

"Oh gods, Mara, you'll wear him out."

"No I won't," she giggled as she petted his newly engorged penis, "he likes it and so do you." She flipped her leg across his body and sat astride his chest, kissed his deeply, then began to slide down his body until she was once again impaled on him. Bracing her hands on his chest, she began to grind her hips in circles, bringing a groan of delight from Jace. His hands reached to cup her breasts, the thumbs gently rubbing the nipples unit they were as hard as bullets.

JACE LAY ON HIS BACK with Mara beside him, her head pillowed on his chest. "Mara?"

"Mmm?"

"This sex thing is one sweaty, messy business."

"Indeed it is," she replied with a grin. "One does wonder why people do it at all."

"I know." He chuckled as he hugged her gently and kissed the top of her head. "Must be a primal thing."

"It sure was for me, but I think we kept the boys awake." There was a deep sigh and a light thump of a tail on the floor at that.

"They can catch a nap tomorrow," he whispered softly. "Sleep now, my pretty lady. I want to hold you while you sleep." She just snuggled deeper into his arms and sighed with contentment. Jace Harper drifted off to sleep, his fondest wish having been fulfilled and in greater measure than he'd dreamed possible. How he did love this woman.

Dreams

Sleep claimed him then, but this time his dreams were different. Once again Jace dreamed of the madman and the witch, but now it was different; he no longer feared the man. The man was no longer fierce and angry, but was old, weak, and trembling with fear of the witch. She, on the other hand was tall and straight, flush with the glow of life and youth.

"It is done, Phidias Tomlinson," she said in a clear ringing voice. "They have consummated the union and are now fully under my protection. You no longer have any influence here. Go."

"You did this, witch," he hissed. "You did this, but it matters not. They will not find it. You may have driven that fool to start this ritual in motion, but he defeated you. He hid the prizes well and they will never find them. We will see how well their love stands up to poverty. When the despair and reality of bankruptcy set in, I will return."

"Go," she replied, pointing a finger away from them.

Cursing, he went, limping as he struggled on every step. When he was no longer in sight, the witch turned to Jace. "You must not fail, Jace Harper," she said in a clear sweet voice. "The power of your new love will let me keep him at bay, but he's not finished. You must find the treasure."

"Which one?"

"Both of them; find the one and you will find the other."

Jace wanted to ask her more, but suddenly found himself in the field where he and Mara had taken the dogs for a picnic. Mara was playing chase with Billy and Scoot. Jace smiled and joined the game. He felt the warmth of the sun on his back and the love flowing from Mara to him and he faded from dreams into deep restful sleep.

Mara O'Grady awakened slowly. Her body was sore, but she was smiling. She was alone in the bed, but it was still warm where he had lain a short while ago. Listening carefully, Mara heard Jace out on the small patio, admonishing the dogs to be quiet and let her sleep. She rose and slid open the window. "Good morning, boys," she sang.

"Good morning, pretty lady," replied Jace. "Want to join us for coffee?"

"Love to."

"You do what you have to, and I'll fix a mug and bring it out for you," he smiled, as he rose to his feet.

"Thank you, sweet man," she sang, as she retreated to the bathroom. A few moments later she emerged from the house in a long, flowing sundress. She sat in the chair beside Jace and moaned with pleasure as she took her first sip of coffee for the day.

After her second sip Mara realized Jace was staring up at the old house. "Jace, are you okay? Are we?"

"I'm fine, honey. We're fine. No more doubts, remember? However, I get the sense we're on the clock."

"What do you mean?" He told her about the dream. "That's pretty much what I dreamed too," she sighed. "What do you want to do?"

"I think we're pretty safe for a few days. I'd like to take some time to get you properly moved in here and spend some time with you and the boys out in the fields. I guess I just want some sort of a honeymoon. I know we're not officially married yet, but I feel like we are. At least, I hope this is how married feels because I like it."

Mara smiled sweetly and reached to squeeze his hand. "Jace Harper, you're a romantic and I love it. That sounds perfect to me, but I don't think we'll get that chance today."

"Oh?"

"Looks like rain," she sighed. "I'd say today is unpacking day for me."

"All right," he grinned. "I'll go on laundry detail after we have breakfast."

"Laundry detail?"

"Yeah, somebody made a hell of a mess in the bedroom last night."

"Yeah," she giggled. "I hope that lamp we broke wasn't a family heirloom."

"Nope; it was here when I got here. All I have for furniture is a hodgepodge of stuff I picked up over the years to fill an apartment."

"Me too. None of it really holds any sentimental value."

"Want to pack everything off to charity and start over?"

"Oh, Jace, I'd love to, but maybe we should wait until the quest is over."

"Okay, that works for me. Whoops, raindrops, let's get in out of it." Rising to his feet he whistled for the dogs. The skies suddenly opened up as they ducked inside. Mara shrieked as both dogs shook the rain from their coats, spraying her with water droplets. Jace began cooking breakfast while she toweled the dogs dry.

They spent the morning in domestic harmony, Mara unpacking and fitting herself into his space. Jace helped and moved the heavy stuff around until she was satisfied. By afternoon the rain had stopped, and they took the dogs out for a walk. Then they went to the big house to clear another bookcase. They found nothing, but enjoyed the peaceful afternoon together, stealing lots of loving glances and kisses.

Eventually they gave it up and returned to the cottage for a meal. Mara was trying to cook and Jace was nibbling on her neck trying to distract her. That's when Jace's phone rang. He pulled it out and thumbed on the speaker. "Harper."

"Mr. Jace Harper?" asked a woman's rich contralto voice.

"Yes, speaking. Who is this?"

"I'm Annie Bell, Mr. Harper. I'm calling to let you know that your cousin Aiden is in hospital."

"What? Where? Is he...?"

"I don't know, Mr. Harper. I just found out myself. I'm in a taxi on my way to the hospital right now. I believe he crashed his motorcycle, but I have no idea of the extent of his injuries."

"Where are you, Annie, which hospital?"

"Springwater Hills, Mr. Harper. It's the Valley View hospital."

"Call me Jace, Annie. Have you informed the others?"

"I've called Morgan Ross, but no one else."

"All right, I'll call the rest for you, Annie. I'm on my way. I'll meet you at the hospital."

Jace turned away and found Mara pulling on her coat. "Springwater is about an hour and a half away, Jace. Shall I drive while you phone?"

"You know the way?"

"Yes."

"All right sweetie, you drive and I'll call the family."

Mara topped up the dogs' water bowl while Jace pulled on a jacket. They rushed out and sped from the driveway. Jace was already on the phone with Ira. They stopped and picked up Ira and Meghan on the way. Just over an hour later they pulled into the hospital parking lot. They parked right beside Morgan's truck.

"Looks like the gang's all here," rumbled Morgan's deep voice, as they hurried down the corridor to the waiting room.

"Any news?" asked Jace, as they reached the others.

"None yet," replied Logan. "Folks, this beautiful lady is Annie Bell. Annie, this is Jace Harper, Mara O'Grady, Ira Dunbar, and Meghan O'Grady. Annie is Aiden's girlfriend."

"I wish," sighed the tall brunette with the face of an angel.

"We'll have a talk with him," grinned Morgan. There was a round of chuckles at that and Annie blushed a deep shade of red.

"Stop it, you guys," chided Mara. "You're not allowed to tease her at a time like this."

"Thank you, Mara," smiled Annie, still blushing.

"They're a bunch of savages, Annie," smiled Mara, "but they're lovable."

"Someone's coming," declared Ira, as he rose to his feet.

The nurse who entered the room was startled and stopped for a second as Ira rose. His resemblance to the movie character Thor was astounding. The sight of the fierce redhead clinging to his arm caused her to step away, blushing. "Mr. Reilly can see you now," she said. "Right this way."

She led them to a hospital room where Aiden, dressed in a hospital gown, was sitting on a bed talking to a doctor. "You're a very lucky man, Mr. Reilly. All that leather armor you were wearing saved you a lot of skin and blood."

"Anyone who rides without leather is a fool," rumbled Morgan's deep voice.

"And my mamma only raised one fool and she's not here," grinned Aiden.

The doctor chuckled at that. "As it is, all I can find is bruising. A visit to a chiropractor to get straightened out should speed up recovery. Take it easy for a couple of weeks and you should be good as new. If you develop any problems at all, come back to see me."

"Will do, Doc, and thanks." The doctor nodded and walked away.

"My god, Aiden," breathed Annie. She was running her long elegant fingers over his shredded leather chaps and jacket. His helmet was there as well, a long split through it.

"Easy girl, I'm fine. The leathers did their job and I'm fine."

"I nearly lost you."

"You'll never lose me, Annie; I promise."

"That brings up another point," grinned Ira. "Annie tells us you haven't asked her to be your official girlfriend yet. What the hell's the matter with you?"

Aiden just chuckled and held his ribs. "Yeah, well, that's where today all went sideways," he said. "As you may have noticed, Annie called you guys; that's because I've listed her as my emergency contact number.

"Annie, I was going slow like I promised, but it was dusk, a car came towards me and blinded me with the headlights for a minute. That's when the deer jumped onto the road."

"You hit a deer?"

"Yes. He's dead, I'm afraid. The folks in the car called for help after I stopped bouncing."

"Define going slow, Aiden." Annie was giving him a hard look.

"Only twice the speed limit?"

"I've seen you ride, Aiden," chuckled Morgan. "You should have been able to clear that one easy."

"How is this relevant to Annie as girlfriend?" grinned Ira. "Get to the point."

"All right," sighed Aiden, blushing. "I was daydreaming of proposing to Annie. I want her for wife, not girlfriend. Happy now?"

"I certainly am," breathed Annie, as she stepped into his arms and kissed him. "If that was an official proposal then I accept."

"And that's our cue to go home," grinned Logan.

They started to leave, but Aiden's voice stopped them. "Hey guys, thanks for coming out instead of just sitting by the phone. It means a lot."

Mara was being very quiet as Jace drove home. "Penny for your thoughts," he said at last.

"Oh, sorry, honey, I was just debating if I should let Annie in on the family sex secret. You know, have a good romp and Gramps can't get at you."

"You think Gramps had something to do with this?"

"Don't you?"

"Yeah, I do. You heard Morgan; he's seen Aiden ride. Aiden used to race those bikes. I really don't see him getting that distracted on the road."

"On the other hand," she smiled, "by the way they were looking at each other it may not be necessary to tell her anything."

"Oh yeah? How were they looking at each other?"

"The same way you and I do," she laughed.

"You mean like two cats in heat?"

"Meow," she purred, sliding her skirt up to show her thighs.

"Stop it," he laughed, as he reached over and pulled the hem of her skirt back down, "I'm driving. Save that until I get you home."

She giggled and laid her head on his shoulder. "Jace, I love you."

"I love you too, sweet Mara. You just wait until I get you home."

"Oh, now that holds promise."

Just then Mara's phone rang. "Mara."

"Hi Sis, it's Meg. We're ordering pizza when we get home, care to join us?"

Mara looked to Jace who nodded his head. "Love to, order an extra 'cause we're hungry. We'll go home and let the dogs out for a pee then come over."

"Perfect; the pizza should be ready by then. Ta-ta."

Next morning Jace awakened alone in the bed. It was late and he'd overslept. He yawned, stretched, then rose to face the day. The dogs jumped up to greet him, accompanied him to the bathroom, watched as he shaved and brushed his teeth, and then followed him out to the kitchen. Mara was there, sipping on a coffee and poring over old maps.

He kissed the top of her head on his way by to the coffee pot. "Morning, lover," she smiled. "Sleep well?"

"Like a baby. You?"

"I did," she smiled. "After all, I was properly tucked in." He smiled at that as he joined her at the table.

"So, what are you up to?"

"I woke up with the strangest feeling I was missing the obvious," she said, as her eyes returned to the maps. "Look at this. This is a hand drawn sketch of the original house Phidias Tomlinson built. We know he had an escape tunnel built and we know it came out near the slave pens.

"Now, the slave pens mysteriously burned down with the slaves inside. I'm betting he set that fire to make sure no living soul would know the location of the escape tunnel."

"What about his wife, the witch?"

"From what I can gather, they kept very much to themselves. It's said she rarely spent a day in that house, but was always out visiting one person or another. She was well known for her healing abilities. It's also said he was afraid to sleep in the same room with her.

"Anyway, here's the sketch of where the slave pens were at that time and here's a map of where the house and cottage stand today. What do you think?"

"It almost looks like the cottage stands on the same site as the old slave pens did."

"Yes, that's how it looks to me too. Do you think...?"

"The tunnel comes out here?"

"Yeah, that. Is it possible?"

"Around here anything is possible," he grunted. "It's raining pretty hard out there. Do you want to explore the basement here today?"

"There's a basement?"

"Well, sort of; more like a cold cellar. It's kinda damp down there so I didn't go poking around, I just left it alone. It wasn't part of the plan."

"You did have a plan, didn't you? I mean, before you actually came here, before we met. You had a plan for the future. What was it?"

"Nothing too spectacular," he grinned. "I'd signed that damned agreement, so a career was out. I figured that, if we could solve it and get all that money, I could set myself up in a swank apartment and live the life of the idle rich. I'd hoped to be able to camp in the old house until I found the stuff, but that wasn't going to work so I moved in here.

"This cottage wasn't meant to be a permanent home or anything, just a campsite. Oddly enough, it's starting to feel like home. Maybe once this is all settled we can take a look at fixing it up. Oh hell, I guess I should be asking what you would like to do?"

"Actually, I like this place. It's cosy, and I do like cosy. Jace, you do understand that if we follow through on making that house a library/museum you'll be stuck here in Higgston."

"Yeah, well," he grinned, "Higgston is starting to feel like home anyway. I like it here. Mara, you're happy in this town. You have family here, and you have friends. I have nothing anywhere else and I'm making friends here; this is fairly close to the other guys, and I like the slower pace of life. Let's stay in Higgston."

"Oh Jace, I'm so happy to hear you say that. I like this town; and I do have lots of friends here. I do want to make that library and museum."

"And write that history of Higgston?"

"Yes, I want to write that history too. So, does this mean we're going into the dark, damp, icky, basement today?"

"Dress warm, sweetheart," he grinned.

Mara held the big umbrella while Jace opened the door to the cellar. Both dogs scurried on ahead while he turned on the flashlight and followed. Mara was right behind, closing the umbrella and shaking the water off. She turned on her light too and began to look around.

"It's not so damp down here, Jace," she said. "This is a cold cellar, you know, for storing winter vegetables and such. See, there's the bins where it was kept up off the floor." She shone her light into one of the bins and found a few old potatoes that had sprouted and tried to produce a plant, but had failed for lack of light. The next one had a few wrinkly old carrots.

"Looks like they stored firewood down here too," he said, as he found a small stack of moldy sticks. As he turned back to Mara he smacked his head on a beam and began to swear.

"Careful, sweetheart, careful," she admonished gently, as she pulled his head down so she could kiss it better, "you don't want to open that wound again."

"No, I sure don't," he sighed. "It itches like crazy and so does the hair growing back."

"I know honey. Judy said it would be itchy as the stitches dissolve. Just a few more days and it'll be all better."

"What's that?" Jace was suddenly interested in something his light had flicked across.

"What? Where?"

"There," he replied as he stepped out of her arms and approached one of the bins. This one had a high back on it. He was playing his light across the floor in front of the bin. Kicking at the gravel he found a hard surface below. A bit more work revealed a small wheel on the leg of the vegetable bin. Jace pulled and the bin grudgingly moved away from the wall.

A large wooden doorway was revealed behind the mystery bin. Close inspection showed that the door was meant to open from the other side. There was no way to open it and the hinges were hidden so it was impossible to take the pins out and remove the door.

"I guess I could get an axe and chop it open," he mused, "but I'm betting the way in there is from that hidden room in the big house."

"This is old. Very old," she mused, as she inspected the door closely.

"How can you tell?"

"The nails are square," she replied, "see here? Modern nails have round heads on them, but the really old ones have square heads. There's no actual mortar around this, just tightly packed stone. We could probably dig the stone away from the door frame, but..."

"That might cause the whole house to fall in on us?"

"Yes, and that would be bad."

"Very bad," he chuckled. "Let's explore a bit more and see if there's a hidden lever or catch or something that might open this baby up."

After about an hour of poking, prodding, and sticking their fingers between the stones they gave up and returned to the kitchen to warm up and have a snack. "Well, what do you want to do?" she asked, as she set the sandwiches on the table.

Jace poured up the coffee and brought it over, setting her mug at her elbow. "Nothing right now, honey. We can't get that thing open from this side, so we're stymied for the moment. However, it does tell us that we're on the right track. Let's have another look at those sketches of yours. Where did you get these anyway?"

"They were in the archives," she replied, as she set her mug back on the table and reached for the sketches. "I made photocopies of almost everything I could find about this place."

"Well then, let's see what other goodies might be hidden in those sketches."

Rain continued to pelt down for the rest of the day. They chatted easily as they pored over her sketches, pausing to watch the storm through the window from time to time. Eventually, they paused for a meal. While Mara was cooking, Jace built a fire in the fireplace. The cottage was warm and cosy in minutes.

"Mara."

"Just a moment 'til I get this pot off the burner. There now, we'll just let that cool for a few minutes. Okay, what was it you wanted to say?"

"Something's all wrong with this," he sighed.

Her world collapsed in free-fall. "Jace?" her voice was soft and wounded.

"What? Oh dear gods, Mara." She was instantly in his arms, his warm lips on hers, turning her fears into joy and lust. "Mara, I wasn't talking about us, silly woman. We've gone way too long without eating something. Let's sit to the table and enjoy whatever that is that smells so good in that pot, and I'll explain what I was talking about."

"Jace, I'm so sorry, I..."

"Carb drop. Depression is a tar pit that hides at the bottom of an empty stomach. We should have eaten a bowl of fruit or something hours ago."

"Is that in the Good Guy's Handbook too?" she asked, as she sat in the chair he's pulled out for her."

"Nope, that's wisdom from the book of Granny Harper," he grinned as he served up the soup and sandwiches she'd made.

"I should have made a proper meal for you," she murmured.

"Can I tell you my darkest secret?" She nodded, wondering what was coming next.

"I've always wanted to learn to cook," he grinned. "Once we have the library/museum up and running you won't have a lot of time for that. How about you teach me a few bits for starters, and I'll become the family chef, take courses and stuff."

"Are you serious?"

"One hundred percent serious, pretty lady."

"Oh dear gods, a man who wants to cook for me? I am sooo marrying you."

"Good, that means my job is safe," he grinned.

"Jace, why did you say something was all wrong?"

"Think about it, Mara, the escape tunnel comes out under the slave pens? If it had been me, I'd want it to come out under the stables for a faster getaway."

"Makes sense to me, but then what the heck is behind that door, do you think?"

"Another tunnel," he replied. "Knowing the kind of man he was, I'd bet the tunnel came out under the slave pens so no one could see him going to the women. I doubt the bedroom was a happy place for him after he caused the death of his wife's sister."

"You said the house is full of secret passageways; do you think the tunnel is actually several tunnels?"

"I'm betting on it."

"So how did he manage to have all this work done and nobody knew about it or where to find it?"

"The slave pens burned to the ground with everybody chained inside, remember? I'll bet the old bastard had the slaves do the building, starting from inside the pens and then killed them all so they could never tell anyone."

"Oh god," said Mara, a shiver running down her spine. "Could anyone be so evil?"

"I'm betting he could," replied Jace, as he set down his spoon and pushed away the plate and bowl. "Mara, that was wonderful and just what I needed."

"Thank you, Jace, you were right, we did need to eat. I'm feeling a lot better now. So, do you think the entrance is in the house?"

"Yes I do. I'm willing to bet the entryway is somewhere in that room where Morgan found me. I think there's been a lot of changes to the original set up over the years as the generations occupied this place. Those sketches give us a good idea of what it was originally like, but I'll bet we find a lot more down there."

"This is exciting and extremely creepy at the same time."

"Still want to marry into a family with history like that?"

"I want to marry you, Jace Harper. Every family has a few skeletons in the closet, never doubt it."

"Even yours?" he grinned.

"Meghan claims to be an Irish witch; what do you think?"

"I think I'm the luckiest guy in the world."

"Oh really? And why is that?"

"It's getting late, close to bed time, and I have you here with me. Life is good."

Mara blushed at the lust in his eyes, and she thrilled to the familiar flutter low in her belly. "Just what do you have in mind, Jace Harper?"

"Tearing off all your clothes and ravishing your body," he replied, as he licked his lips, causing her to blush even deeper.

Suddenly she leaped to her feet with a, "Gotta catch me first," and fled towards the bedroom. Jace jumped up to chase her and the dogs began to bark wildly, getting in between them. These were big dogs and could be dangerous if things got out of hand. Both Jace and Mara stopped and began to sooth them.

"It's all right guys, we were only playing. I know, it's been a boring day for dogs and it's not fair to play without you guys getting in on the fun. Jace, have we got anything we could use for playing tug-of-war?"

"I've got a couple of old towels," he replied. "Just a minute. He retrieved the towels from the linen closet and tied a knot in each end. He tossed one to Mara then offered one end of his to Billy. Billy knew this game well; he grabbed the knotted towel and began to pull. Jace was startled at the dog's strength as they pulled each other across the room and back.

Mara was laughing as Scoot dragged her around. It took all her strength to get stopped and put up a reasonable fight. The humans soon tired of the game, but not the dogs. After a rousing game of tug, Mara lay in Jace's arms, breathing deeply. Jace had already flopped onto the couch. Meanwhile, Billy brought his towel to Scoot and they were now pulling each other around, growling and making fierce noises while their tails continued to wag.

"Mara."

"Mmm?"

"About that ravishing; I don't think I have the energy anymore."

"Oh, poor baby," she soothed as she lightly kissed his lips. "You just rest here on the couch and regain your strength." Suddenly she got a mischievous twinkle in her eye. She pushed her hand down the front of his jeans and grabbed his penis in her hand. She began to squeeze him rhythmically. "Hi, my name's Mara and I'm from the heart foundation," she giggled. "I'm here to check your pulse."

Jace laughed and groaned at the same time. Mara struggled with his belt for a moment then got it loose, unzipped his pants, and pulled him out into the air. "There now," she said. "That's better. Uncle Wiggly was suffocating in there. See how happy he is now? I know poor Jace is all tired out, but you'll help me, won't you Uncle Wiggly?"

She rose to her feet and began to dance a slow striptease, tossing her clothes aside and shaking her bare breasts at him. "Like what you see, Uncle Wiggly?" she teased.

"Oh gods, does he ever," groaned Jace, as he struggled out of his jeans and T-shirt.

"Now, you're too tired for this, Jace," grinned Mara, as she pushed his slowly back down onto the couch. "You just lie there and rest while Uncle Wiggly and I deal with my little problem."

Jace groaned as her hand gripped him tightly and her warm mouth engulfed him. His hands began to wander over her body, but she stopped him. "Oh no, Jace, you're much too tired for that," she grinned, gently pushing his hands away. She turned to face him and straddled his chest. "You just rest there while my little friend and I take care of this.

"Uncle Wiggly, I have an itch deep inside, can you scratch it for me?" she purred, as she began to slide down his body and impale herself on his raging hard on. "Ohhh," she moaned, as she engulfed him once again, "that's it, just a bit deeper now." She slid further down him. "Almost there, can you reach a little further?"

As she spoke she pulled out one of his chest hairs. Jace yelped and thrust up at her, driving himself fully into her body. Mara groaned with pleasure. "That's it woman," he growled, as he grabbed her butt and began to thrust up at her, "now you're going to get it."

"Oh good," she panted, "cause I really want it." She tangled her fingers in his chest hair and held on, riding the bucking bronco beneath her.

They lay exhausted, Mara still on top of him. "Jace?"

"Hmmm?"

"Are the dogs still playing tug-of-war?"

"Huh? Oh, yep, they are."

"Oh, okay. I was hoping that was them growling and not Uncle Wiggly."

Her breasts jiggled against him as he shook with laughter. "No dear, Uncle Wiggly has absolutely nothing at all to growl about."

She giggled at that. "Well, it's good to know he's happy with me."

"He's thrilled with you, my darling. So are the boys; they're using your jeans for the game of tug."

"What??? Hey!" She leaped to her feet to see the dogs drop the knotted towel to the floor. They looked at her contritely, not sure of what they had done wrong. "Aw, sorry guys," she soothed, as she gave them each a scratch behind the ear. She turned and pounced on Jace. "You sir, are a complete rotter."

"Yes," he chuckled, "I guess I am at that."

"Well, you have to make it up to me. I'm going to shower; you have to come with me and wash me all over then tuck me into bed."

"Can I ravish you in the shower?"

"Only if you're up to it," she grinned.

"Now there's a challenge I can rise to," he laughed, as he rose to his feet and gathered up their clothes to throw in the hamper. She already had the water running when he reached the bathroom. Smiling with delight, he stepped into the stall and took her in his arms. He kissed her softly. "I love you, Mara O'Grady," he breathed, as their lips slowly parted.

The Door

J ace awakened to the sound of distressed dogs. He stretched, yawned, and then rolled out of bed. With the dogs dancing ahead of him, he headed for the door. They burst through to do their business and Jace stood on the step, basking in the morning sun while he waited for them.

Loving arms encircled his waist from behind and he was hugged tightly. "Good morning, my love," he smiled, as he hugged the arms that held him. "Did you sleep well?"

"I sure did," replied Mara. "You?"

"Yes, ma'am, I did indeed."

"Is there coffee?"

"Not yet, the boys had an emergency brewing."

"I heard that," she laughed. "I'll go start breakfast; shall we have it on the patio?"

"Sure. I'll grab a towel and dry off the furniture."

The breakfast dishes sat empty on the table, and they were enjoying a second cup of coffee. "So, what's on the agenda for today?" asked Mara.

"First, the boys need a good run then I want to go back into that hidden room, set up lots of light, and search for the hidden door to the tunnels."

"Sounds good, but I'm a speed walker, not a runner. You guys go play and I'll take a walk in the sun."

"We'll go with you, sweetheart. The boys are getting old, and I'd rather walk than run."

"Seriously? Then why..."

"I wanted to be able to catch that damned burglar. Man, for a big guy he sure could move."

"In his line of work that would be an advantage," she laughed. "Okay, we take the boys for a walk, then we go door hunting. Sounds like fun to me."

They walked in the sun, hand in hand, chatting happily about their plans for the old house and the museum Mara wanted to make. They also talked about the history of Higgston she wanted to write. Jace said he just wanted to make Mara's dream a reality for her; that was his dream.

Once they returned, Mara stayed with the dogs while Jace went to the hardware store. He soon returned with several long extension cords and powerful work lights on stands. He also had a generator, just in case Gramps found a way to kill the power again. Jace wasn't taking any more chances.

The afternoon was well advanced by the time he had everything in place the way he wanted it. He spent the rest of the afternoon moving everything in that room away from the walls. Jace checked everything he found thoroughly before carrying it upstairs and dumping it into the big garbage bin outside.

While Jace worked on the secret room, Mara worked in the Library. She was down to the last bookcase and still hadn't found anything close to what they were looking for. Eventually they gave it up for the day and returned to the cottage.

The next day they both went into the hidden room and began the search for the hidden switch. They didn't find it, but Billy and Scoot found the hidden door. Mara sighed deeply and leaned her back against a beam.

"Tired, honey?" asked Jace.

"Yes," she replied. "But I'm not ready to give up. Jace, what are the dogs doing?"

He turned to see both dogs snuffling at a spot where the floor and wall met. "What have you got, guys?" he knelt beside them and ran his hand along the floor by the wall. He almost missed it, it was so faint, but it was there.

"There's a draft here," he grinned. "The door must be here. Good work, men." He hugged and wrestled the dogs and they wagged their tails furiously as they each tried to lick his face.

Laughing at their antics, Mara joined them and placed a large piece of tape on the wall just above the draft. "Okay, we have a starting point at last," she smiled. "Let's go home and have something to eat."

"Good idea," agreed Jace. "It's getting late. Let's end today's search on a positive note and come back at this tomorrow."

"I approve of that plan," said Mara, as she started up the stairs. They shut off the lights then locked up the house and went home for the day.

Next day they were back, searching for the trigger that would open the door. They found nothing. "Jace, maybe we're looking in the wrong place," sighed Mara.

"What do you mean? Where else would it be?"

"Upstairs in the study, maybe?"

"Damn, I hadn't thought of that, but you could be right. Let's go see what we can find." It was there, just inside the hidden panel in the wall. Mara pulled on a projecting piece of wood that looked like a broken away part of the house construction; it moved easily. She pulled harder and they heard a grinding sound from downstairs. Hurrying back down the stairs, they found the hidden door open a crack.

Jace worked his fingers into that crack and heaved. The door gave way and opened a bit farther, but it seemed to be hitting something. "Some of the old earthen walls must have slipped in blocking the way," he muttered.

"No, Jace, wait. Look, here's another lever." Mara reached for the handle she saw just inside the hidden door. It was easy to tell what it was now. She pulled down and the door slid open the rest of the way.

Jace flicked on a flashlight and stepped through the opening. His second footfall triggered the booby trap and a piece of the roof fell in on him. Mara screamed and tried to pull him out, but he stopped her.

"Mara, get back. Mara, get back out of here. My foot is caught, but I'm afraid you might get caught too if something else falls. I should have known the old bastard would have this place trapped. Damn that man to hell anyway."

"Jace, what should I do? I can't leave you here. I'm going to call the fire department."

"No, Mara, no. We don't want to spread this around and we don't want dozens of heavy handed men in here messing things up. Just give me a few minutes to see if I can work my way loose without pulling the rest of the hill down on my head."

Mara stood in the entryway, wringing her hands and trying not to panic while her lover struggled and squirmed under a pile of stone and rubble. Suddenly she saw him lurch ahead. She leaped to grab his hand and pulled as he lurched again. Another moment of struggle and he was free.

Jace stood swearing as he beat at the dirt clinging to his clothes with one hand while holding Mara tightly with the other she was crying and trembling. "Oh Jace, I was so scared. What are we going to do? This place is so dangerous."

"Yes it is, honey. I really am working up a serious dislike for Gramps. I think we've reached the point where we need reinforcements."

"Reinforcements?"

"Logan used to work construction. He's our best bet to figure out this tunnel."

"You can call him while I'm patching you up," she sniffed, as she regained some composure. "Can you walk?"

"No problem," he lied, as he limped a few steps.

"All right, let's leave this and go home where I can clean you up and make sure you're all right."

Leaning gently on her arm, Jace limped down the hill to the cottage. Stripping off the dirty and tattered clothes he discovered several scratches and lumps that would make painful bruises, but, besides the sprained ankle, he had no major damage. While Mara fussed over him and prepared dinner, Jace called Logan and explained the problem.

"Well, I'm no structural engineer," said Logan, "But I'm sure I can figure out a few simple traps. Listen, I've found what I need here, and this isn't a friendly town. I've got a good offer for this place; you interested in new neighbors?"

"Are you serious? It would be great to have you in Higgston."

"Okay, I'll come down tomorrow and have a look at your tunnel, and Renee can go house hunting."

"Thanks, Logan. See you tomorrow."

Next day Logan arrived and introduced Renee, then Mara took Renee for a tour of the town while the men went underground. It took them most of the day to clear away the rubble from the cave in. The girls returned with pizza and drinks, then abandoned them again. Finally Mara returned alone.

"Hey there, happy miners, Renee is cooking up a storm at the cottage. You guys hungry?"

"Famished," sighed Jace, as he straightened up and rubbed his back to get the kinks out. "Logan, you get the shower first; you did most of the work."

"Awesome," replied the younger version of Jace, "that means I get to the table first."

"Forget that," chuckled Jace. "I'm eating your share while you clean up."

"Stop it boys," chideded Mara. "Play nice. Believe me, there's plenty of food for everybody."

They were tired, but happy as they locked up and headed back to the cottage. Once the men had showered and were ready Renee put enough hot food on the table to feed a dozen people.

"Renee, that was delicious," sighed Jace, as he pushed away his empty plate and leaned back in his chair.

"Amen to that," agreed Logan. "The girls cooked, Jace; you know what that means."

"We're on clean up?"

"Ah-huh."

"Works for me," grinned Jace, as he rose to his feet.

"Not today, Jace Harper," said Mara, as she took his arm and steered him toward the sofa. "You and Logan earned your dinner today. I'll clean up, but first I want a coffee and the story of what you two managed to discover today."

"You're a good woman, Mara O'Grady," smiled Jace. "I'm keeping you."

"Good, because I do want to be kept. Everybody relax in the living room and I'll bring the coffee."

Once they were all settled, Mara posed the question. "Well, Logan, what's the verdict?"

"It was a booby trap all right, Mara," he replied. "That tunnel was really well built and built to last. The original guys must have had mining experience. Anyway, it wouldn't have come down unless it was meant to."

"So, is it safe now?"

"I doubt it," said Jace. "That was just the entrance. I'll bet there are several more traps in those tunnels."

"Tunnels? As in plural?" asked Renee.

"Tunnels, as in plural," replied Logan. "We didn't explore very far, but we did find where it split into two separate directions."

"Like you said, Jace," smiled Mara, "one to the slave pens and one to the stables for a fast getaway."

"Logan, my friend, we are the children of a long line of nasty people," sighed Jace.

"Yep, that we are. So, do we follow tradition, or do we try to balance the scales?"

"We balance the scales."

"I was hoping you'd say that," chucked Logan.

"Oh? Why?"

"Because that's a lot harder, and I always seem to enjoy doing things the hard way." Renee giggled at that. "So, what's on the agenda for tomorrow? Do you want to go on, or do you want to wait for the other guys?"

"I want to go on a bit further," replied Jace. "I'd like to be sure the passageways are safe before anyone else goes down there. Will you stay and help?"

"Love to, besides, Renee will need more time to house hunt."

"No, darling, Renee has already found it," she smiled. "Eight acre hobby farm set up for horses, new barns and a poorly renovated old farmhouse. Tomorrow I'll research the local market, but I believe the price is right. The house will need a lot of work, but that's what you wanted, right?"

"Yes, my girl, it is. However, before we go putting a down payment on it, we need to help the other guys find their part of the map. You got kicked out of your home once; I won't ever let that happen again."

"Not to worry, Logan," smiled Jace. "If even half of the things described in those old journals is down there then we're all set for life anyway."

"Thanks, Jace. I'm just thinking of the good we could do with all of the treasure."

"Agreed. So, horses?"

"I love 'em," sighed Logan. "I want to start a riding stable for folks with physical handicaps."

The rest of the evening wore away in friendly speculation and dreams of a better future. Eventually Jace and Mara retired to bed while Logan and Renee claimed the fold out couch.

The next morning, as the men set out with the dogs leading the way, Renee called to them. "Gentlemen, take this with you, it'll save you a lot of time and energy." She was holding out a straw broom.

"I don't understand," said Jace, as he accepted the broom from her hand.

"That nasty old man went to that storehouse of treasure many times," she replied. "Probably generations of them walked that path. I truly doubt any of them stepped on a trap. Sweep away the dust and you should be able to find their path around the traps."

Jace grinned and kissed her forehead. "Logan, this woman is a genius; keep her."

"I absolutely will," grinned Logan. "I have to; she's the brains of the outfit."

Mara and Renee were still smiling with delight as the men and dogs headed up the hill to the old mansion.

By nightfall Jace and Logan returned with broad smiles and stories to tell. They had found the path just as Renee had said. It led them to another wooden door with a huge lock. It also led them to another entryway hidden in the overgrown hedge halfway down the hill. A bit of poking around showed up the remains of a stone foundation. This had been the site of the stables.

"This is really exciting," said Mara as they gathered in the living room for coffee after dinner. "Are you going to open that door tomorrow?"

"Nope," replied Jace. "We're going to take a couple of days to figure out the traps and disable them."

"How?"

"They're simple lever traps," said Logan. "They pretty much have to be. We've located the places where the old bugger avoided stepping, so we know where the triggers are. We'll shore up the roof over those spots then carefully root out and disable the triggers. We don't want anybody else getting hurt down there and Jace says he wants us all to be there for the grand opening."

"Jace?"

"I promised we'd all share in the treasure if there is any, and I meant it. So, tomorrow you girls can contact the others; tell them to come ready for anything."

It took a couple of days to make the place safe and by then it was Tuesday evening. The next day the rest of the family would arrive, and the mysterious door would be opened at last. The excitement was rising and sleep was late coming that night. When it did, bad dreams followed.

Behind the Oak Door

Next morning Jace rose early to feed the dogs. He was vaguely aware of them soothing him in the night. By the time he finished, the others had gathered in the kitchen and the coffee was brewing.

"Fine, if no one's talking about it, I'll go first," sighed Mara. "I was haunted last night, how about you guys?"

"Oh, yeah," sighed Logan. Renee nodded her agreement.

"Old Gramps was giving it full guns last night, all right," said Jace. "The witch tried to hold him off, but he was giving it his all. Personally, I think we're really close and he's starting to panic."

"Yeah, I have to agree," said Logan, "but we worked hard the last few days, and we didn't get a lot of sleep last night. That means we're tired and it means we go extra slow and careful today."

"I agree, Logan," said Mara. "I don't want either of you getting hurt." Just then her phone rang.

"Mara. Seriously? All right, put the coffee on, we're on our way."

"What's up?" asked Jace.

"Arlene's cooking breakfast for the treasure hunters and then Aunt Louise is taking over the coffee shop so Arlene can join us for the big reveal. Morgan and Ira came into town last night and Aiden is on the road. He'll be at the café in about half an hour."

"Is Annie with him?"

"I'll be surprised if she isn't," giggled Mara.

They arrived to find Morgan and Arlene sitting to a long table that already had the coffee set out. "Now that's service," grinned Jace, as he lowered himself into a chair beside Mara. Ira and Meghan arrived just then and a few moments later, an old luxury car pulled into the parking lot. Aiden got out and walked around to help Annie.

"Aiden, where's the crotch rocket?" asked Morgan, as they joined the group.

"Still in the shop," sighed the tall man, as he held Annie's chair for her then sat beside her. "I doubt it'll pull through. They've tried life support, but..." Everyone was laughing at that point.

"Nice car," observed Logan.

"It was cheap and in good shape," replied Aiden. "I asked no more of it. Once we get squared away a bit we'll get Annie a decent car."

"You going for another bike?" asked Ira.

"Nope. My racing days are over. Now I want a truck like Morgan's."

"Finally, a man with taste," grinned Morgan.

"Aiden, you did say you wanted to get a touring bike," smiled Annie.

"Yes, my love, we'll get a touring bike and see the world together."

"Hey, come on you guys, you're driving me crazy," Arlene said excitedly. "What have you found? Anything? What are we looking for today?" The entire café had instantly gone silent as she spoke. "Oops, sorry."

"It's all right, Arlene," said Jace. "I guess it won't hurt to let the cat out of the bag now. We've found a hidden tunnel under the old house. It was booby trapped, but we made our way to a thick reinforced oak door. Today we're going to bust the lock and open that door. I know there're a lot of legends about treasure up there, but knowing what a real bastard old Gramps was, I doubt it. He probably cashed it in long ago. We're more likely to find a torture chamber."

"Order up!" came a call from the kitchen.

"That's us," said Morgan, as he and Arlene rose to fetch the food.

"I'll help," said Meghan, as she followed them to the swinging doors. Soon the table was laden with food and the happy buzz of voices as they ate. When they finished, the waitress Arlene had called in for the day gathered the dishes and brought more coffee.

"Arlene, stop fidgeting," chuckled Mara, as they enjoy their coffee.

"I can't help it, Mara," she said. "I'm too excited. Come on, everybody in town has speculated about that treasure all our lives. Today we find out if it's real or not. Aren't you the least little bit excited?"

"Nope, not me."

"Liar," grinned Arlene, as she gently poked her friend in the ribs.

"All right, family," smiled Jace, as he rose to his feet and offered his hand to Mara. "Let's go put Arlene out of her misery. It's time to see if we can bust open that door."

"I'll bring my lock picks," grinned Ira.

"Lock picks?" asked Meghan.

"My step dad was a locksmith," he replied, "I grew up working on locks."

They stepped out of the café to find a group of people gathered and waiting for them. Cameras and cell phones flashed and calls of *happy hunting* rang out. It was clear they were the latest in a long line of treasure seekers.

"There's nothing up there," called one old fellow. "If there was old Jake would have found it long ago."

"Who the hell is Jake?" asked Logan.

"He was caretaker up there for twenty years," replied the old man. "He searched that place every day and never found a thing."

"Is that a fact?" rumbled Morgan. "Now that is disheartening. Think I'll just give up and watch you guys make fools of yourselves and then write the book." That brought a round of laughter from the gathered folks.

Jace just grumbled something sarcastic and held the car door open for Mara. He pulled out and led the way for the others. When they arrived at the old mansion they saw a few cars had followed them. The curious onlookers parked on the side of the road a way back, not wanting to interfere or be accused of trespassing.

"Damn it to hell, I didn't want this to turn into a bloody circus."

"Relax, honey," smiled Mara. "They're just curious, that's all. They don't mean any harm."

"If you say so," he sighed. "Come on family; let's get in out of the spotlight."

They filed into the old house and stood in the vestibule. There was definitely a creepy feeling and they all felt it. "Forget it, Gramps," grinned Ira. "I have the tools right here and today we open the magic door. You lose."

"This way, folks," said Jace, as he led the way to the study. The secret panel was open with two heavy duty extension cords running through it. "Just give me a minute to get the lights on." He turned on a powerful flashlight and went through and down the stairs. Bright lights came on and the stairwell was no longer dark.

"Be careful," said Mara, as she led the way, "these steps are old."

"Those steps go to hidden passageways?" asked Annie, as she reached the secret room under the house.

"Yes," replied Jace. "They go all through the house, complete with peek holes so the old buggers could spy on everybody."

"Creepy," she observed. "This whole place feels creepy."

"Indeed it does," agreed Renee.

"This way," said Jace, as he indicated the tunnel. "Logan and I've disabled all the booby traps so it's safe."

"You sure you got them all?" asked Morgan.

"Yeah, pretty sure," replied Logan.

"That's a comfort," sighed Morgan.

"We got them, Morgan. It's safe for Arlene to go in," replied Jace. "Do you think I'd let Mara or any of you go in if it wasn't? Come on."

The tunnel was barely over six feet high and the men all had to hunch a bit, but Jace and Logan had strung lights so the passageway was well lit. It wasn't far to the huge wooden door.

The door was made of oak with iron bars across it fastened with carriage bolts, the nuts on the inside so they could not be removed. It would have been nearly impossible to chop through it with an axe. It was fastened shut with a huge old lock.

"All right, Ira," said Jace. "There's the lock; do your stuff."

"Okay, let's have a look then," said Ira, as he knelt at the locked door. "Wow, this is an old beauty; real museum quality. It shouldn't take long." He opened a small roll of tools, chose two, and began to poke and prod at the lock. A moment later it snicked and he popped it open then passed it to Mara. "There you go, Mara; the first relic for your museum. It's all yours, Jace."

Jace lifted the latch handle and pushed. The door screeched in protest as it was pushed open, but it gave way. Jace stepped inside with the others crowding close behind. What they found wasn't what they'd expected. This wasn't a treasure room; it really was a torture chamber. There were chains with manacles hanging from heavy beams and others anchored in cement on the floor.

There were branding irons, tongs, and several bladed weapons loosely piled on a bench which stood near a brazier. There was an iron cage that was too small for a human to stand upright in and another cage with dozens of sharp pointed pegs pointing inwards.

"Jesus Christ," breathed Jace.

"Doubt he was ever here," said Morgan. "This looks more like Lucifer's den to me."

"You're right there," said Mara.

"This place is seriously creeping me out," said Annie, as she tucked herself under Aiden's arm.

"So, what now, Jace?" asked Logan.

"Now we put our thinking caps on," he replied. "We go out and show the watchers that we found nothing, and then we retire to the cottage for a coffee. We put our thinking caps on and decide what to do next. Come on."

They returned to the house and exited by the back door. They waved to the gathered onlookers who laughed and began to disperse. Once gathered on the patio and relaxing with coffee, Jace spoke again.

"All right, family, that was a bust. Your thoughts, please?"

"I think we quit too soon," said Morgan. "You've got those journals that list all the goodies; the treasure has to be somewhere down there."

"I agree," said Mara. "Does the other tunnel go anywhere? What about the one under the cottage?"

"The one under the cottage can only be opened from the other side," said Jace. "I say we leave that on the back burner for now. If everything else comes up blank, then we break it down and go at it from this side."

"I think Morgan's right, Jace," said Meghan. "I mean, there were traps and a heavy lock guarding that room. Why?"

"Meg's got a point," said Ira. "Why go to all that trouble to guard a torture room that likely hasn't seen use since the days of slavery?"

"You think there's another room hidden behind the torture chamber?" asked Arlene.

"Yes, I do," replied Ira.

"I agree," sighed Jace. "Here we go again. Let's make certain our audience has gone home, and then we can have another look at it."

The onlookers had left, so they climbed the path back to the old house and returned to the torture chamber below ground. Carefully, they began to inspect the room, searching the walls for a hidden door. They found nothing and after a couple of hours gave up. Jace was clearly disappointed.

"Logan, why would they go to all the trouble of a wooden floor in here?" asked Ira, as he ran his fingers through his long golden hair in frustration.

"You're right," replied Logan. "It doesn't make a lot of sense, does it?"

"Okay, everybody except Ira back into the tunnel," declared Mara. "Ira, you're the heaviest of us, walk every inch of this floor until you find a soft spot."

"Yes, ma'am," grinned the young giant. It took him less than ten minutes to find the trap door under a loose bench. It was made of heavy planking, but it did give slightly under his weight. Once he was watching for it, it was easy to find. With a shout of victory he moved the bench away and pried up the trap door. As the door swung upwards it revealed more steps going down.

The others crowded back into the room and Jace passed a big flashlight to Ira. "Take a look, Ira."

The beam of light played around in the hole for a moment then he switched it off. "Another tunnel," he grunted, "probably trapped."

"My job," said Logan, as he approached. He was holding the broom Renee had brought for them. She grinned and winked at him. Logan moved carefully down the steep steps then began to carefully inspect the tunnel. It was quite short, ending at another door like the one above.

Suddenly they heard the sound of metal snapping and Logan cursing. "Sweet Jesus, I fucking hate that old bastard."

"Logan!" screamed Renee.

"I'm all right, Ren. I'm all right," he called. "Or I will be as soon as I get some clean underwear."

"What happened?" called Jace.

"Bear trap," growled Logan, as he returned to the bottom of the steps. "The old bastard had a bear trap set down here. The dirt didn't look quite right so I poked it with the broom handle. It scared the crap out of me when it sprung. That would have easily broken a man's leg.

"You can come down now; it's clear."

One by one they descended the stairs, slowly filling the short passageway. The door was locked with a similar lock to the one above. Ira had it open in a jiffy, but this time the door did not want to yield. He put his shoulder to it and heaved. Grudgingly, it gave way. "Now this looks a lot more promising," he said, as he swept the beam from his flashlight around the room.

They all entered, filling the room with the lights they carried and casting ghostly dancing shadows all around. Morgan brought up the rear, dragging a powerful standing work-light and extension cord behind him.

"Now that's better," grinned Jace, as the big light illuminated the room and exposed everything to view. About twenty feet long and ten wide, the room resembled a bank vault. The left wall was lined with shelves containing metal boxes like safe deposit boxes in banks. The right wall was covered with metal cases with smaller drawers like jewelry drawers in the big shops. Every box was locked.

"All right, now we look for the keys," sighed Jace.

"Got 'em," sang Renee.

"How???"

"The floor dips a bit right here," she smiled, "and this drawer's handle is more worn than the rest. Look, two keys, I'll bet all the big boxes are keyed to one key and the smaller drawers on the other side to the other key."

"Here's the ledgers," said Mara, as she pulled a set of large books from the top of one shelf. "As I guessed, this lists what every drawer and box contains."

"Find your ring, Mara," Jace said softly.

Everyone held their breath while Mara accepted the keys from Renee and walked along the bank of small drawers. She stopped at one and tried the smaller key. It worked and she slid the velvet lined drawer open. There were several rings inside, each tagged with a number. She selected a magnificent diamond ring and handed it to Jace.

Jace Harper smiled with delight as he gazed at the ring she'd dropped in his hand. He rubbed it on his shirt to shine it up a bit then reached for her hand. "Mara O'Grady, will you marry me?" he asked.

"All right," she grinned, "but it has to be tomorrow, you promised."

"A promise I will gladly keep, my darling," he smiled, as he slipped the ring on her finger. He pulled her close and kissed her gently to the cheers and cat calls of the others.

"All right folks," smiled Jace. "I promised to share this find and I will. I've just claimed my prize, now each of you choose something for yourself, then we'll lock her up again and go back to the cottage for coffee and figure out how to divide this all up.

There was a round of thanks and congratulations as they set about exploring some of the boxes and drawers. In the end, the men each chose a ring for their lover and the women were content with that.

"I'll bring the ledgers," said Mara, as they exited the vault. "We can use them to figure out how to split it all up."

Ira locked the door behind them then changed his mind, swiftly picked the lock, and tossed it aside. "You need new locks."

Jace nodded his agreement as he helped Mara climb back up the stairs.

This time they gathered in the kitchen for coffee and snacks. Mara flipped through the ledgers as she took a sip of her coffee. An envelope fell out of one and she looked at it with a puzzled expression. It was addressed to Jace.

Jace looked at it for a long moment then tore it open. There was a note inside. He read it aloud. "Jace Harper, I am surprised that you managed to get this far, but the real treasure isn't here. You might survive by selling off the old fool's trinkets, but your cousins will kill you if you back out now.

"I guess it's only fair to give you a hint, seeing as how you managed to get this far. What you're looking for is on the library. Good luck finding it.

Grandfather Miller"

"Sorry Gramps," grinned Jace, "but you've really misjudged the quality of my cousin/brothers. Mara, how much of the library is left to go over?"

"Just one more bookcase, lover; we should be able to go over it in less than a day."

"And if we all help?" asked Meghan.

"A couple of hours, easy," she smiled in reply.

"All right," grinned Jace. "Let's have a bit more to eat then hit the library. I want this over with. We're getting married tomorrow."

As they reached the house, the dogs bounded on ahead. They knew their job and enjoyed it. By the time Jace reached for the door handle Scoot popped out of the doggy door, wagging his tail in the all-clear signal. Jace gave him a quick rub then they all made their way to the library.

The women pulled the books from the last of the bookcases and Ira and Jace lifted it out of its position against the wall. While the girls organized the books the men inspected the bookcase and the wall behind where it stood.

"Nothing," sighed Jace, as he and Ira set the big bookcase back into place.

"Then we're down to the books," said Mara, in full librarian mode. "Each of you choose a row of books. Here's what you're looking for." She went on to explain how she and Jace had been doing it before. They set to work with a will, examining each book very carefully. Two hours later they had found nothing and it was finished.

Jace opened his mouth to swear, but Mara laid her finger to his lips to stop him. "We're not done yet, my love. We have several more options in here to explore."

"We do?"

"We do, but I've been avoiding it."

"Why?"

"Because I love books, especially old books, and damaging one gives me the shivers."

"Damaging one? Why would we damage one?"

"Jace, there were several books in here that had been repaired. I made notes of them and especially the ones with the thick leather covers."

"You mean you think it might be..."

"Hidden in the cover of one of the books, yes. I have my notes and a very good idea where I filed them as we put them back in their cases. It may take a few days to locate and inspect them all, but we will do it."

"My magical Mara," he sighed, as he pulled her into his arms and kissed her forehead. "Sorry guys, I guess the hunt goes on here, but we did find Old Miller's treasure. Let's go back for a meal and see if we can decide how to divide up that pot of gold."

Jace locked up and followed his family down the hill to the cottage. "What's that smile for?" asked Mara, as she linked her arm in his.

"I always wondered what it would be like to be part of a large happy family. I think I have my answer and I like it. In truth I think this is the real treasure."

"I love you, Jace Harper," laughed Mara. "You're such a softie."

"Well I'd have to say that's a good thing, Miss O'Grady, because you're marrying me tomorrow."

They'd finished a meal and cleaned up afterwards. Mara had been shooed off to inspect the ledgers. The rest had sat around, sipping coffee and speculating on their dreams and aspirations for the treasure. "How's it coming, sweetheart?" asked Jace, as Mara sat back to rub the kinks out of her neck.

"Well, as near as I can figure there should be several million dollars each here, but it is hard to say for certain. There are a lot of stocks and bonds, but I have no idea if they have any value or if those companies still exist. I know some do. I'm just hoping the actual papers haven't deteriorated too much over the years.

"There are several boxes of actual cash, each marked with the totals of the contents. There are fifty-three gold bars, eighteen platinum bars, and all the jewelry. There are also one hundred and sixteen rare coins that will have to be evaluated. He has estimates for that value here, but we need to have each piece inspected and evaluated again. There's no telling how long this stuff has been down there."

"It looks like this isn't going to be as easy as I'd hoped," said Jace. "Okay, first thing tomorrow we split up the cash then we head for the gold exchange in the city. We cash in the metals then come back and divide up the rest. We can all take away a share or, if you're willing to trust me, I'll cash all that stuff in and split with you all."

"We've trusted you so far," chuckled Morgan, "and it's done nothing but good. This is your show, Jace. I'll happily enjoy whatever you want to share, but I'm content to have you divide it up." There was a round of agreement at that.

"There's something else we should do and soon," said Aiden. "If the locals see us carrying tons of stuff out of that house they'll know we found something. You could have a lot of curious trespassers."

"Great," sighed Jace. "What do you suggest?"

"You said there's a door under this place. Find the tunnel that connects to it and bring everything out through there. Folks will be watching the main house, not the cottage."

"I like it, Aiden, but the tunnel dead ends under what must have been the stables."

"So we missed something. Look, none of us are really hurting for cash at this point. We had fun treasure hunting, I was able to get a really great ring for Annie, and I'm content for now."

"You're saying we should re-focus on the original quest?"

"I am. Once we have that beaten, we can revisit those tunnels at our leisure, right?"

"That makes sense, Jace," said Morgan.

"Does that work for everybody?" asked Jace. It did.

"All right, but know that your share is here if you need it, all of you."

"Thanks, Jace," said Logan. "As soon as Ren and I get settled into a new place I can hang out in those tunnels and see what's what."

The next day, they all gathered at the court clerk's backyard and witnessed Mara and Jace get married officially. "So, going on a honeymoon?" asked Meghan, as the congratulations continued.

"Not yet," said Mara, as she hugged Jace's arm tightly. "As soon as the quest is completed, Jace has promised me a big wedding and a honeymoon. For now, the quest goes on." She gazed again at her hand and the way her diamond sparkled in the light of the afternoon sun. Jace had stopped at the jewelry store to buy them matching wedding bands. She smiled as her sister kissed her cheek and congratulated her again.

EVERYONE HAD GONE THEIR separate way and the newlyweds returned to the small cottage that was their home. They were greeted enthusiastically by the dogs who wheedled a walk out of the happy couple. As they were returning, Mara spoke to the thoughtful mood Jace seemed to have fallen into.

"Penny."

"What?"

"Penny for your thoughts," she smiled. "I was just wondering where you went."

"Oh, I didn't go far," he smiled as he put an arm around her shoulders. "I was just thinking about us and the quest."

"Oh?"

"Yes. It's all different now. I feel more settled. Having you beside me takes things away."

"Things like?"

"Fear and doubt?"

"Tell me?"

"Mara, when this mad adventure started I signed a contract that swore I would never work again. Up until that point I was always driven, always climbing higher over the bodies of those in my way. In short, I was the man Gramps would have been proud of.

"I became determined to avoid that fate at all costs and become a better man than my ancestors. It is easy to make than resolution, but a lot harder to live up to it."

"Of course it is, but you're doing a marvelous job of it, lover." She squeezed his fingers and gave him that smile that sent his heart a flutter.

"It is with you beside me, Mara. Sadly, when I first approached you for help I had something very different in mind."

"Oh? What was that?"

"Finish the quest, pass you the deed to the property, then head for the South Seas or some other place to find myself. I really had no clear idea at all of what I wanted to do."

"Has that changed?"

"You know it has," he smiled, as he took his arm away and unlocked the door. He carried her across the threshold and set her gently on her feet, then kissed her softly. "Now I know what I want to do. I'm so much happier with a game plan."

"So, what's the plan?"

"The plan, my darling wife, is to finish the quest, help you set up that library/museum, then help you run it. That'll give you time to write that history. It will also give me lots of time to read."

"Jace? Honey, I've never actually seen you reading a book."

"We've been far too busy," he sighed. "When I was so hell bent on getting out of debt, I would often stay home and read instead of going out. It was incredibly relaxing, and a library is a lot cheaper than going to the bar with the other guys."

"Didn't you want to meet girls?" she teased.

"I've always had a fetish for librarians," he grinned. "You don't find a lot of them in the bar."

"You're a nut, Jace Harper," she laughed. "So, what's on the agenda for the rest of the day?"

"I'm going to cook for you then, after we eat, I'm going to carry you into the bedroom, strip off all your clothes and make mad passionate love to every inch of your body." He grinned. "At least that was my plan. Did you have something else in mind, Mrs. Harper?"

"Oh, that can wait, Mr. Harper," she breathed, as she stepped into his arms. "I like your plan a lot better."

THEY'D FALLEN ASLEEP entangled in each other's arms. Jace had been as good as his word and Mara had floated on a sea of passion and ecstasy before being cuddled to sleep in the arms of her new husband. She awakened a few hours later to the sounds of Jace struggling in his dreams. She tried to wake him, but the voice in her head stopped her.

"Mara, leave him; he has to face this alone."

"Get out of my head," she snarled, as she continued to shake him gently, "You're not supposed to talk to me until I call for you."

"Leave him be, Mara."

"I didn't call you; get out of my head."

"Stop it, Mara. The time for your childish foolishness is gone. There is great danger, and you need to be ready. We need to talk. Leave Jace to fight this battle, for fight it he must, and he must do it alone."

"But he's..."

"Battling his own nature, child. You can't fight this one for him and neither can I. However, the time will soon come when you'll have a battle of your own to fight."

Mara rose and padded to the kitchen for a glass of water and to clear her head. "All right, talk to me," she said, as she settled into a chair and sipped at the water.

"The men are drawing closer to solving the riddles the old madman set out for them. What he didn't know is that I managed to cloud his mind enough to make him hide something else."

"Oh? What was that?"

"The means to banish his spirit forever. He's a lot stronger than I thought, Mara, and his fear is making him stronger. I can't hold him in check much longer."

"What do you mean, the means to banish him forever?"

"It's a short but powerful ritual, Mara; to be performed on the very spot my sister took her life. The five men must be there with five good and true women. I have been working throughout your lives to bring all five couples together. Each woman has been chosen to be completely compatible with the man she chooses. This is a spell that must be cast by love if it is to banish the evil that destroyed love so long ago."

"Why the hell didn't you ever tell me any of this before?"

"I tried, but you went crying to your mother. She packed you off to that idiot who put you on drugs so you couldn't think straight. I told you to keep my voice secret, but no, you had to..."

"All right, I get it, I screwed up. So what do you want now?"

"For you to be happy," sighed the voice, "and that will never be possible as long as Phidias Tomlinson has an influence on this world. At this moment he's badly weakened, but not gone. He is now focusing all his energy on your husband, working away on that part of Jace Harper that's connected to him. Jace must win this struggle on his own."

"He will," Mara said firmly. "What happens after that?"

"You find the key and the clue. The clue will be a line from the spell. Once all the pieces are found, you will be able to put it together. The map will lead you to the place. The keys are the old man's bank account numbers, nothing more."

Suddenly there was a shout from the bedroom and Mara ran to her husband's side. He was sitting up, soaked in sweat, and trying to shake off the cobwebs. "Jace, honey, are you all right?"

"Yeah, I'm okay. Jesus, what a nightmare."

"Tell me," she said, as she sat on the bed and took him in her arms.

"It was like before," he said, as he kissed her forehead and snuggled her close. "The old man was there, and he had you chained to a wall. It was down in the torture chamber we found. I could hear the witch on the other side of the door, but she couldn't get in. He hit you with the whip and you screamed.

"I went crazy all over him then and he went down, but he got back up. Mara, when he got up his face had changed. It was me. *'Face it, you young fool,'* he said. *'This is what you truly are. Stop fighting it and enjoy the wealth, the screams of the women, the tears and begging of the beaten...'"*

"Oh Jace..."

"That's when I hit him again. I didn't care whose face he was wearing, I had to put him down. We fought for quite a while before I figured it out."

"What?"

"The fight was what he wanted. As long as I fought him, he had my full attention and could pull me into his world. I stopped fighting him and just looked at you. He hit you with the whip again, but you held my eyes and didn't feel the pain. I stepped in front of you and the whip hit me, but I didn't fight back. I unhooked the chains from you and carried you out of there.

"He tried and tried to get me to fight him again, but I just ignored him. When we stepped through the door of the torture chamber he screamed and vanished. The witch appeared beside us and healed our wounds with a touch of her hand. She pointed back into the torture chamber and we looked. There was nothing but a pile of ash where he should have been, and I yelled in victory. I think I woke myself up.

"What do you think it all means?"

"I think it means you beat him, sweetheart," she smiled as she gazed lovingly into his eyes. "I tried to wake you from that dream, but couldn't. The witch wanted to talk, and she said you had to fight that battle alone. Here's what she told me..."

"Wow, so she's behind the whole thing, the quest, I mean. The old man's fortune was just the incentive to get us involved, to meet her chosen women, and to perform the ritual to banish the spirit of the man who caused her sister's death, to complete her revenge."

"Yes," Mara said softly, as she withdrew slightly from his arms. "Now that you know, do you want me to leave? You were tricked into this whole thing."

"Leave? Mara, what the hell are you talking about?"

"Jace, you were tricked into this marriage. I'd be angry if I were you."

"Are you?"

"Am I what?"

"Angry? Do you want out?"

"No, oh gods, no, Jace, I love you. I..."

"Me neither, silly woman," he smiled, as he pulled her close and kissed her softly. "Mara, you're the best thing that ever happened to me. I don't care how we were brought together; I'm just thrilled the fairy godmother chose such a perfect woman for me. Girl, I will never willingly let you go, not ever. You're my wife and I'm keeping you."

He lay back on the bed and pulled her down to him. He kissed her softly and snuggled her close. They drifted off to sleep again and this time, he didn't dream at all.

They awakened late and took their time getting breakfast. That was followed by a long walk with the dogs. It was afternoon when they returned to the library to pick up the quest. They had barely started gathering the books Mara had singled out on her list when the phone rang. It was Morgan.

Jace put it on speaker. "Harper."

"Jace, it's Morgan. I've got it."

"Got what?"

"The map and clue, Dummy. I've got my piece of the puzzle."

"Morgan, that's awesome. Where did you find it?"

"I didn't, the other guy found it for me."

"All right, Mister," laughed Mara, "stop teasing and talk."

"Yes, ma'am," chuckled Morgan. "I was a bit late getting back from Higgston, as you might imagine. When I reached the house a guy came blasting out carrying a huge box of stuff. Man, for a big guy with his arms full he could sure run. It took me a while to catch him, but I finally brought him down.

"I convinced him to give me the box and then let him go. The bonanza was in a small tin in that box of stuff. It had the piece of the map, a note with some gibberish on it, and a check for another quarter million."

"Morgan, save the gibberish," said Mara. "It's the most important part."

"Oh yeah? I'm listening; talk to me." Mara told him about the conversation she'd had with the witch.

"So we have to banish the old bugger to finish this, do we?" growled Morgan. "That works for me. Jace, you had to fight the old bugger yet?"

"Last night. You too?"

"Ah-huh. Took me a while to figure it out, but it went easy after that. Haven't had a nightmare since."

"When was this, Morgan?"

"Last week."

"Why didn't you tell us?"

"I meant to, but with the treasure hunting, house hunting, and all I just forgot."

"House hunting?"

"Yeah, Arlene loves her little café, her town, and all her friends so I'm moving to Higgston. I hear Logan is too."

"Morgan, that's wonderful," said Mara. "I have the sense this will all end here anyway, and I'd love to have you guys as neighbors."

"All right then, I'll go put the For Sale sign on the gate and head out your way. You guys get busy and find that damned clue. I really want to banish that old bastard forever and the sooner the better."

"Second that," sighed Jace. "See you soon."

They set to work then, gathering all the books that might hold the treasure. Mara swallowed hard as Jace took out the sharp knife he'd brought for this task. Seeing her face, he paused. "Mara, I know it pains you to desecrate a book this way, but we have no choice."

"I know; it's just that some of these are quite rare and in excellent condition. I know it's silly of me, but I just can't help it."

"Can they be repaired afterwards?"

"Yes, if we're careful."

"Then we'll be very careful, my darling." Having made the promise, Jace carefully cut the stitches on the old book's bindings and peeled back the cover. He found nothing. He sighed and reached for another. Two hours later there was a stack of books with flapping bindings on the long table and no treasure.

"Mara, I am so sorry for this. I would have sworn it was in one of these."

"I know, Jace; I thought so too. Let's go home and get something to eat and decide on our next move."

"Good idea, honey. Billy, Scoot, let's go." Both dogs were instantly awake and heading for the doggy door at the back of the kitchen. Outside they waited to escort their humans back to the cottage.

"Dammit all to hell and back," growled Jace, as he finished his meal and pushed the plate away, "we're missing something. Let me see that note the old swine left for me in the treasure room."

"Here, sweetheart," smiled Mara, as she passed the note to him. "He said it was in the library. I should have known he lied."

"No, Mara, he didn't say it was in the library," mused Jace, as he stared at the paper in his hand. "He said it was *on* the library."

"On the library? So what does that mean?"

"That means there's another hidden space in that house."

"What???"

"There's got to be an attic with a hidden access," sighed Jace, as he set the paper down beside his coffee mug. "That's the only thing I can think of."

Mara set her mug back on the table and shook her head sadly. "We've searched that place from top to bottom. Where in the name of mercy are we going to look for the next hidden stairway?"

"It has to be somewhere in those passageways we found. I don't feel like crawling through all those creepy passageways today. I'm still a little tired from last night. I say we go to bed early and catch a few hours' sleep and then tackle this new search in the morning."

"I agree my love," smiled Mara, "but it's a bit early to go to bed, isn't it?"

"Too early to sleep, maybe," he grinned, licking his lips as he stared at her breasts.

"Mr. Harper, behave yourself," she admonished in her best annoyed librarian voice, as she crossed her arms over her breasts protectively.

"Oh, hell no," he breathed, as he began to rise from the chair.

Mara shrieked and leaped to her feet. She fled, to the bedroom with Jace in pursuit. He caught her and spun her around. Laughing, she came to him as he grabbed her butt and lifted her high. Mara locked her legs around his waist and kissed him deeply, hungry for his mouth, his body, his need for her.

"Mara, do you remember my favorite fantasy?" He breathed into her hair as the kiss ended.

"Oh yeah. Does my hungry man want dessert?"

"Indeed he does," he replied, as he lowered her carefully to her feet then began to undress her slowly.

They began with Mara leaning against the wall and moaning with delight as she tangled her fingers in his newly grown hair. They ended with her lying on top of him in the bed, asleep. He eased her to the sheets, keeping her tucked close against him, and then closed his eyes. Jace Harper had the first peaceful night's sleep in many days.

Morning came bright and sunny, and with it a renewed hope. They walked the dogs, ate breakfast, and then set out for what they hoped was the final push to their piece of the puzzle.

"So, where do we start?" asked Mara, as she tossed her sweater across the back of a chair in the library.

"Well, we've been over every inch of this library," mused Jace. "If it was in here I'm sure we would have found it by now. Let's grab the flashlights and check out the passageways from the hidden room."

Nodding her head in determination, Mara led the way to the study. The door to the tunnels was closed and while she retrieved the flashlights, he triggered the hidden catch. Jace dragged the long extension cord through the door and down to the hidden room. A moment later it was flooded with light. "All right, let's start here with the steps going up."

"I'm right behind you, sweetheart. Please be careful; I don't want you to fall."

"I fall for you every day, Mara my delight."

"Fall for me all you want," she replied tartly, as she swatted his butt, "just don't fall on me."

"Such a big difference one little word can make," he chuckled.

"Indeed, like on the library instead of in the library."

"Yep, just like that. Okay, here's the end of the line here and here's the peek hole." He put his head to the wall. "I'm looking down into the first floor of the library." He pulled back and they both began to play their lights around the small narrow passageway. They found nothing and eventually gave it up. Two more passageways explored later, and nothing to show for the adventure except being covered in dust, they gave it up and went back to the cottage for lunch.

"We've eliminated all but one of the passageways," sighed Mara, as she reached for the fresh mug of coffee he'd set before her.

"Then that has to be the one," he replied, as he gathered the dishes and put them in the sink.

"I sure hope so," she replied, taking another sip.

"Me too," he replied, as he ran the sink full of water and splashed some dish soap in with it. "As soon as we find that damned map, I'm going to buy us a decent house."

"What's wrong with this one?" she asked. "I like it here."

"There's no dishwasher," he grumbled.

"It would be a lot cheaper to have one installed." She was smiling with delight at their playful banter, and he fell for her all over again.

As if drawn by a magnet she rose from the table and floated into his arms, her lips seeking his as his arms enfolded her. When their lips parted he pulled her tighter and whispered her name. "Mara."

Her lips moved close to his ear and her soft seductive voice whispered to him. It was not what he expected to hear. "There's pirate treasure to be found, Mr. Harper," she breathed. "Look lively now."

"What???"

Mara shrieked with laughter and tried to wriggle out of his grasp as he tickled her. "I'm going to get you for that," he growled with mock ferocity.

"Oh gods, I hope so," she laughed, as she escaped.

"All right," he sighed. "Let's go get this done so we can get on with our lives. I want to stop this foolish treasure hunt and spend a few months ravishing you in a thousand different ways."

"Oh, be still my dancing heart," sang Mara, as she opened the door for the dogs. She placed her hand in his as they followed the dogs to the big house.

Flicking on the flashlights they began to ascend the last of the stairs into a narrow passageway. It went up a dozen or so steps, then they had to duck under a beam. There was a blood stain and some hair stuck to the timber. "This must be where I smacked my head," he mused.

They ducked past the beam and the passageway ran flat for several feet. At the end it turned a corner and went up again. They reached the top and it ran flat again, then another turn and up once more. There was a trap door at the top. It was locked with a combination lock like they'd had in high school. "You've got to be kidding me," snarled Jace.

"Now what?" asked Mara. "I don't think I can get this one with the stethoscope."

"No, but I can with a crowbar. Let's go back and get one."

They returned slowly to the hidden room where Jace located the crowbar Logan had left behind. "What are you doing, sweetheart?"

"Replacing the batteries with fresh ones," replied Mara. "I brought lots of extras when we went into the tunnels. I'm not taking any chances here."

"How I do love a practical woman," grinned Jace. "Let's go get that damned map; I know it has to be up there. Why else would that trap door be locked?"

"That makes sense to me," she smiled. "I'm ready when you are."

Jace accepted a light from her hand then led the way back up to the trap door. "Stay back, Mara," he said, as they reached the last set of stairs.

"I'll wait right here at the bottom until you tell me it's safe."

"Kiss me for luck?"

"Luck, my darling," she breathed, as she locked her lips on his.

As their lips parted he held her tight. "Gods, Mara, when you kiss me like that I forget my own name."

"Your name is husband, now go break that lock for your wife, the burglar."

"With extreme pleasure, my beloved wife," he grinned.

Jace approached the lock carefully, as he was still standing on stairs and didn't want to take another tumble. Setting down the light, he worked the claws of the crowbar into the curve of the lock and heaved. After a few mighty heaves the lock remained intact, but the hasp that held it broke free and gave way. Jace pushed the door upwards and tossed the broken lock mechanism inside. "Come on up, sweetheart."

"Right behind you," said Mara, as she swiftly climbed the stairs and followed him into the attic.

The room was low, and they couldn't stand upright. Playing the lights all around they saw dozens of small boxes and tins stacked everywhere. "Aw crap," sighed Jace. "It'll take us days to go through all this."

"You knew it wouldn't be easy," she said, as she opened a tin to find several ancient photographs. "You know, I'll bet we have the beginnings of a museum right here."

"Do you want to take it all downstairs to the library before we start going through it?"

"Yeah, I do," she replied. "Everything here is covered in years of dust and my back is already hurting.

"All right, let's get started." Jace picked up a couple of small boxes, blew the dust off them, and then handed them to Mara."

"I can carry more than this."

"Not if you're carrying a light too. We'll take a small load now and I'll string some lights on the way back up so we can have both hands free."

"Such a sensible man," she grinned. "Is it any wonder I married you?"

"None at all," he smiled, as he lightly kissed her forehead. "We were made for each other."

They worked diligently the rest of the day and the next two days as well. First they carried everything down to the hidden room in the basement, and then carried it up to the library. Finally they were ready to start opening boxes. It took two days to go through the boxes only to come up empty.

"Dirty, rotten, egg-sucking, son of a bitch," growled Jace, as he tossed aside the last of the boxes. "I hate that nasty old man." He got to his feet and marched away.

"Jace, where are you going?" called Mara, as she hurried after him.

"To check the one place we didn't look yet," he replied, as he triggered the hidden panel in the study.

"Where's that?" she asked, as she followed him down to the hidden room where he flicked on all the lights.

"Behind the damn door of the attic."

She followed him up to the tiny room where he lowered the trap door behind them. There was a brown manila envelope stapled to the back of that door. It had his name on it. Mara held the light for him as he tore it open and shook out the contents. There was the note addressed to him, a check for two hundred fifty thousand dollars, and a piece of a hand drawn map.

"Gotcha," exulted Jace, as he began to read the note aloud.

"Well, well, well, Jace Harper, you're made of the right stuff after all. I truly didn't expect you to find this. However, you did, so here's your prize, another check in case the others can't come through, a piece of a riddle that must be solved, and one fifth of the map to the ultimate prize.

Good luck,

Grandfather Miller"

"Don't try to make sense of the riddle, Jace," said Mara. "That is actually part of the spell. I doubt he even knew what it really was. We have the prize. Let's go down where we can stand upright."

Jace Harper was almost in a trance as she led him back to the library. They had detoured to lock the map and rhyme in the treasure room, keeping out only the check. "Jace, honey, are you okay?"

"Huh? Oh, sorry, sweetheart, I guess I'm in shock. I've devoted my life to this search for months and now it's over. I guess I thought I'd feel a great sense of victory or something."

"Instead you're just hungry."

"What?"

"It's a blood sugar drop, sweetheart. We haven't eaten for over six hours. Come on, the boys and I will take you home and feed you. Once you're all powered up again, you can call the others with the good news."

"You know," he grinned, "I think you're right. How did I get lucky enough to marry such a wise woman?"

"Oh, you think you're lucky do you?

"Oh yes ma'am, I do indeed think I'm lucky."

"Well, Mr. Harper, if you think you're lucky now, just you wait until later tonight."

His laughter was full and rich, and it lifted his mood. Suddenly he swept her into his arms and swung her around and around. "We did it, Mara. We beat the old bugger. We found all his secrets."

"Yes we did, my love," she laughed, "yes we did. We beat him at his own game."

After the Find

The next few days were a bit of a fog for Jace Harper. Mara was starting to worry about him. She finally broached the subject when she found him sitting on the ground with the dogs asleep at his side.

"Jace?"

"Mmm?"

"Honey, are you okay?"

"What do you mean?"

"You seem lost," she said, concern in her voice, "and you're sitting on the ground staring into space."

His laugh was full and rich. "I guess this is a bit strange all right. I was playing tug of war with the boys and my mind just wandered off. They must have fallen asleep waiting for me to wake up."

"What's wrong, lover?" asked Mara, as she sat beside him and leaned her head against his shoulder.

"People have always said I was too driven," he replied. "It's not that, though, because I'm not. Not really. I'm just very goal oriented. First it was school, then it was my job and paying off my debts, then it was the quest. I guess I'm just feeling a bit lost. I mean, it's all down to Aiden and Ira now; all I can do is wait."

"Well, since it is a wife's duty to think of things to keep her husband busy, I'll have to make you a list. There are several things you can do right now to help steer our fate. You can go help Ira or Aiden, you can sort out the Miller treasure, or you can help me start putting the library in order."

"There's something else I can do too," he replied, as he put his arm around her shoulders and pulled her close. He kissed her tenderly, but she began to pour some passion into the kiss. Just then the phone rang. Chuckling, he pulled it from his pocket.

"Harper."

"It's Ira, I've found it, Jace. I'm on my way to Higgston right now. I'll stop by the bank, transfer my account and deposit the check, then I'll bring the map to you. I've already called Meg; we're going house hunting."

"You're moving here too?"

"Yep, gotta keep the family together. See you in a couple of hours."

For some reason that call seemed to bring Jace out of his blue funk. He stood and took Mara's hand to help her to her feet. "You know, this is all going to work out." He smiled as he pulled her into his arms. "I'm a goal oriented man, Mara. As long as you can do your duty and keep me moving towards one goal or another, I'll be just fine. Let's go get a start on that library of yours."

For the next several days they worked on the library, getting it set up for public use. Jace hired a landscape contractor to clean up the outside and set up a parking lot as well as a picnic area. This was kept to the front of the building and hedging was planted to keep the back private.

Mara worked steadily in the library, even going so far as to dress in her personal librarian suit, as Jace called it. Professional cleaners were brought in to clean up the inside, but the study and secret passageways were off limits. Jace cleaned the study and claimed it for his own private space. He even bought new furniture and a couch for reading by the window.

All seemed like domestic bliss, but Mara knew he was troubled. Jace was doing everything in his power to keep his mind busy, but the quest still weighed on him. His dreams had changed too, and he had reluctantly confided in Mara.

"Another nightmare, Jace?" she asked one morning, as they shared breakfast on the patio. It was autumn now and they were in sweaters to keep off the chill. "Care to share?"

"All right, sweetheart," he sighed. "It's Gramps. He's haunting me again, only now it's different."

"Different how?"

"He's not trying to bully me anymore. Now he's trying to win me over. You know, telling me how rich I can be if I let him help; stuff like that. The thing is, a couple of years ago I would have probably gone for it. Now it just sickens me."

"Oh?"

"Mara, I have nothing against being rich," he sighed. "I actually like the idea." She giggled at that. "The thing is, I don't want it at the expense of others. Sadly, I was well on the way there when all this happened. Now I can't get that burglar out of my mind. He was once a hard working productive citizen; now he's reduced to being a scavenger to survive.

"No, I don't want to be the cause of that, and that's what Gramps is trying to rope me into. I know he just wants to get back into somebody's head, but it sure isn't going to be me. The problem is, I'm losing sleep and getting tired. It's wearing on me, and I just want it finished so we can enjoy our lives."

"I understand, honey; honestly I do. I guess he's leaving me alone because I'm already living my dreams. There's nothing more he can offer me."

"This is living your dreams, Mara? We're stuck here in limbo with this old house and a small cottage instead of a proper house. This is your dream?"

"My dream is to be married to a man who loves me for who I am, bodyfat, nuttiness, and all. I've always dreamed of this, and having a great library, and the leisure to write that history."

"Don't forget the museum," he grinned.

"Yes, and the museum too. Jace, as far as I'm concerned, I have it all. What are your dreams?"

"I don't have any, Mara. All I ever dreamed of was getting out of debt and staying there. Actually, now I dream of finishing this damn quest and putting Gramps in ghost jail, or wherever he's going to go. Once we get this done maybe then I can think of something." Just then Scoot nudged his hand.

Looking down and smiling, Jace scratch gently behind a furry ear. "You think so, Scoot?" he said, smiling at last. "Maybe old Scoot has the right idea. Way too many of his kind are put down every day and there's no need of it. Maybe we can finance a no-kill shelter and retirement home for old dogs. That sure would keep me busy."

"That's the key here, isn't it, darling," smiled Mara. "You need something worthwhile to keep you busy. I have that with my projects, but they're not really your dreams. You need a few of your own."

"You're right, honey. I guess I do..." The phone was buzzing. Jace pulled it from his pocket.

"Harper."

"Jace, it's Aiden. Got it. Annie found the last piece of the puzzle for us. Since the whole family is moving to Higgston, we thought we'd join the group. We'll hold up in the motel for a week or so while the lot of us put this thing to bed. I want it over and done with so I can get on with making Annie an honest woman."

"Aiden that's the best news I've had in a while. Have you called the others?"

"Nope, you're the first. Annie can drive while I work the phone. See you in a couple of hours."

Mara was amazed at the change in Jace. He was alive again, his eyes fierce as he leaped to his feet and shook his fist at the house on the hill. "Did you hear that, Gramps? We've got all the pieces now. You're going down."

"Now there's my husband," smiled Mara. "Jace, it's good to see you all fired up again."

"Mara, I'm sorry to be such a wet blanket these past few days. This thing has had me consumed. I promise to be a better husband to you in future."

"Oh my darling," she said, as she rose to step into his arms, "I have no complaints."

"Mara," he breathed, as he nuzzled her neck and planted soft kisses on her delicate skin.

"Mmm? Oh, don't stop; I like that."

"Are you going up to the library this morning?"

"I was," she replied dreamily, as his lips continued to caress her throat.

"Are you going to wear that librarian suit?"

"I was," she replied softly, rolling her head to give him better access to her neck.

"Please do both."

"Mr. Harper, what are you up to?"

"Fulfilling another of my favorite fantasies."

"Tell me more," she moaned softly.

"Well, I've always thought it would be amazing to make love to a librarian right in her own library. We've got a few hours until Aiden gets here..."

"You're a delightfully sick man," she giggled. "All right my lover if that's what you want. I've often had a similar fantasy."

"Oh yeah?" he breathed, as his lips began to trace the swell of the breast just below her throat. "Tell me."

"Well, it's your favorite fantasy, only in the library," she moaned.

"Mara, I'm shocked."

"You're not," she replied, as she rose up on tiptoe to snuggle his face between her breasts. "You want to; you know you do."

"Oh god, do I ever," he admitted, as he swept her into his arms and carried her inside. "Hurry up and get your suit on." He set her down and swatted her butt to send her on her way. She giggled as she danced towards the bedroom.

A few moments later, Jace headed for the old house on the hill with his demure librarian on his arm. "We'll fix your wagon, Gramps," he thought, as he unlocked the door and ushered her inside. "We'll finish this damned quest then fill this old place with enough love to keep you away forever."

As Jace and Mara made each other's fantasy come true, a beaten and malevolent spirit brooded and gathered strength for the final battle, and his ancient enemy gathered her forces around her. They would make an end of him, and her vengeance would be complete.

The End

Don't miss out!

Visit the website below and you can sign up to receive emails whenever Jenni Leigh publishes a new book. There's no charge and no obligation.

https://books2read.com/r/B-A-XWWCB-NPAUC

BOOKS 2 READ

Connecting independent readers to independent writers.

About the Author

Jennifer Crandall is a reclusive writer who writes under three names, Jenni Leigh, Prudence MacLeod, and JL Crandall. She also writes in several genres.

Far away on a windswept island she sits with her dogs, cats, and coffee weaving stories that take you away from the care of this world for a while. Come enjoy the adventure with her.